DONALD TRUMP

THE BRAVEST MAN IN THE WORLD

OVERCOMING ALL ODDS & EVIL – FOR AMERICA!

DR. LIONEL SWISSON

The investigative journalists Simple Snoopy and Learned Lewis, with no political affiliations and leanings report on the saga of the leadership and bravery of former president Donald Trump. Commencing their investigations as neutral and unbiased researchers from the end of 2023 to July 4th, 2024, into the presidential political race, they found the one-sided injustice deliberate and unprecedented in the annals of American history.

The triumph over adversity is also unparalleled and they called Donald Trump the Bravest Man in America. A lesser mortal would have folded in the face of the unimaginable and shockingly conscienceless sustained political mischief he has had to fight against. The strength and resoluteness in his leadership may be the urgent need for the Americans to securely prosper at home and for the USA to reclaim its vaunted place of freedom and entrepreneurship, and be the Land of the Free and the Home of the Brave!

Table of Contents

Introduction and Brief Background

This is the reporting story of two investigative journalists Simple Snoopy and Learned Lewis. Their research commenced as independent and unbiased research exponents, with the aim to understand the awareness and knowledge of law and politics of everyday people. In the course of this engagement, their focus was on simultaneously imparting education to foster critical thinking and displaying an appreciation for the political ideologies of the principal political parties in the country.

In these communications, be prepared to recover quickly from speech that may be coarse, rude, impolite, innuendo laden, insulting, and other forms of bluntness. The duo responds to the insults hurled by the other side and are penchant to call a spade a shovel, figuratively to not mince words, and to ask and tell it all, as it is. A one-sided discourse is counter-productive to expanding the boundaries of education and knowledge in relation to the upcoming presidential elections, and marching on from the setbacks the nation has faced during the inauspicious rein of Joe Biden.

As this project progressed, the stance of being purely independent was ever so slightly deviated from, as the findings from the ongoing research began to increasingly indicate one-sided weaponization and an abundance of out-and-out hate by one side. Therefore, in response, Simple Snoopy and Learned Lewis started to see what was good for the country, and not about political leanings or support for one political party or another, perhaps a reinvented form of journalism of good versus evil, and with a difference!

Chapter 1:
The United States and It's Perilous Future!

The United States of America is universally considered the Greatest Nation of Earth. It is the Land of the Free and Home of the Brave – unless a President(s) apologizes on the world stage, and belittle us – take a guess, who did this recently?

The welcoming nature of the country is unparalleled. It's success is due to the magnificent contributions, presence, and representation of individuals as citizens and those aspiring to be, from virtually every nationality and race on earth. The remarkable good, wonderful achievements, and the finest traditions of a country are, however, easily undone by a political party and weak leadership, leading to its detriment, as is the current situation in the United States.

The political persuasions of the political parties in major democracies around the world fall broadly under two ideologies: liberalism and conservativism, without delving into the nitty gritty here. In the United States, the Democratic and Republican Parties correspond closely with liberal and conservative ideologies. This broad classification largely holds true for the major parties in the United Kingdom, India, and several other countries, albeit with different names and some variations of these philosophies.

The twin aims of leadership in most democratic and other countries are to ensure the continued economic prosperity and progress of its citizens, and to preserve the integrity of its borders from illegal entry and the consequent violation of its laws. Threats to its identity and such aims led to the UK leaving the European Union, after a referendum vote to do so as Brexit officially took place on 31 January 2020. Pakistan has deported over 375,000 Afghans since late 2023. China is an impregnable fortress, impervious to outside migrations, and India does everything to prevent illegal entry from Bangladesh, Pakistan, Nepal, and swimmers from Sri Lanka.

In the United States, people should realize that the integrity, economic prosperity, and success of its people and the sanctity of its border are not narrow-minded and evil conservatism. It is simply common sense, safety and good for the country and all those who live in it. Let not a party and hate detract from your ability to see what is good versus evil. The interests of the wonderful people living in the country are good policies first, and Nasty Politics by Evil Politicians last!

The sanity and logic in economics and secure borders, universally favored, are of great current trepidation and concern to the vast majority in the United States. A disservice to the people of the country; it is clearly the combination of stupidity, hidden agendas, and vested interests by the ruling party and its leadership. The weaponization against the former president, Donald Trump, will also be explained in this book, along with the sad state affairs prevailing in the United States. The situation will be irretrievably lost forever unless people opt for a change in leadership in November 2024!

Another Biden term will give him false confidence, as he will unhesitatingly and ignorantly get rid of many of the fine traditions of the United States with the stroke of a pen and 'Executive

Orders" on Day One, and of course, continue to unleash and enact further detriment in the course of four more years of abject failure.

No Sequence and Chronology in Fiendishly Evil Perpetrations

There is no sequence and logical flow of events in this book, as the many events criss-cross each other. The reason is simple: ruinous evil is not an orderly and chronological process. It does not follow a schedule. Evil means, the crooked transgressors do damage, at every twist and turn, turn impatient and order the courts – Hurry it Up!

The descriptions, stories and analyses in the book make it conducive to read any page and return to unread sections – little stories unto themselves, within the larger spell cast, that radiates across the Hub and from the core spindle and 'Axle of Evil.'

Aside from the main characters, the two investigative journalists, Simple Snoopy and Learned Lewis, are forced to defensively engage in arguments, debates, trading of insults, name-calling, disparagement, and stingily vicious barbs and attacks, often with scant regard for decency. Advocates and champions for right vs. evil, their comebacks are educational, humorous, and with gusto!

The two investigative journalists reveled in probing and finding solutions also with no method in the madness. Featured on the cover are President Trump and the Evil Monster, with the smaller inset images showing the principal, cloaked in Evil, with his armed Disciples, frequently referred to as the 'Axle of Evil' in this book. The back cover of the book shows the Main Evil and the Second Witch in Command. Not for the faint of heart, but all in Fun and Good Spirits!

Make no bones about it, but we are one Nation under God, indivisible, with liberty and justice for all. Our fervent plea in this book is to:

a) Amend positively laws, phrases, texts, and ideals, which have served as well, however now need slight change for the better, to reflect existing realities. For example, "justice for all" can also be bad and weaponized justice brought upon us, many say, which, if not checked, will be disastrous for our future. The Pledge of Allegiance of 1885, when the population of the United States was 63 million in 1890, is vastly different from the internet era of 2024, with the current estimated population of the United States being 341 million.

b) Restore our value for allegiance, pride, and respect for country, people, and flag!

The Musings are a series of political opinions of the experts Simple Snoopy and Learned Lewis.

We trust the reader can see that despite the wickedness in the weaponization uncovered against Donald Trump, legal astuteness, critical thinking, and a higher level, humor, satire, and kindness are effective tools to de-fang the Evil Monster and derail the Axle of Evil!

"Pleased to meet you, hope you guess my name

But what's puzzlin' you is the nature of my game."

Well, we do have profound sSympathy for the Devil, as the Rolling Stones have requested, the head of the Empire, of our country, and we know the nature of the game. **Please see the introduction to the unveiling of Evil below, and throughout this book:**

The Truth Uncovered from Artful Investigative Journalism

This is the story of two investigative journalists, **Simple Snoopy,** and **Learned Lewis,** looking into the most important decision we will make in our lifetimes in electing the next President of the United States in November 2024!

Simple Snoopy and **Learned Lewis** are both on a mission to engage in discourse, wherever invited or uninvited, in social media, in public and private gatherings, and in forums and meetings. Their aim is to discern current levels of common sense, legal and other knowledge, critical thinking and how informed are these laymen audiences on the contestants of the 2024 Presidential elections, their policies, and what they are going through.

The Profile of Simple Snoopy

The personalities of Simple Snoopy and Learned Lewis are vastly different in their outlook and approaches to the craft of journalism. Simply Snoopy is impish and gives back as good as he gets, perhaps at times aggressive and often crosses the line of civility, but largely in response to the aggression of the other side, in good and bad taste. You could think he pioneered the doctrine of Both Sides Now Journalism.

His concern is educating and ridding people of their ignorance or, at the very least, provoking them to go back to study, introspectively reflect, and be ready to make informed choices and decisions in the elections. His mantra is Policy, not Person in making prudent choices at the ballot. He says, 'Take your blinders off, the lenses of party and political biases, as it impresses me when you can dispassionately look at both sides of an issue, argument, or a candidate.'

An Example of Simple Snoopy at Work

The sale of Bibles for $60/- each was in the news, a little before Easter 2024. As usual, it was met with the expected questioning of the motives of the former President Trump. Many called it an insult to Christianity, using religion and giving it a bad name, and much of the same. The intensity of hate and nastiness increased with each success, as he had just warded off the ridiculously astronomical bond by the evil conspiratorial duo of Ergonomic and Lettuce.

Each success also swelled the number of his voters, and had an equal and opposite in wooing new voters, based on what I am seeing. Droves are coming on board. Joining in are African-Americans who can relate to his discrimination, Latinos who can see the better days in retrospect, and the country – the fair-minded and those dispassionately seeking happier times. The unflappable loyalists and most Americans are now seeing the writing on the wall with the continuance of the *status quo,* and more determined than ever to uproot the Axle of Evil and the Empire!

Tales of Braveheart

'Trump selling his Bible immediately led to outcries on social media of sacrilege, blasphemy, manipulation, desecration, anything but giving credit for the innovative business idea, relevant when the crime is up, morality is down, and heathens are pouring into the country across our southern and northern border,' said Herman, the Hermit.

BUT WAIT, said the next aspirant to the Billy Mays pitchman throne! Order in the next 2 hours and receive a free recording of Cheeto Jesus singing his version of the old Southern Baptist classic hymn- "How Great I Art."

Actually, pure jealousy that Trump's ideas outwit those of so many from the dislike mob. But suppose Joe tried to sell a Bible, he'd likely fumble his way through the pitch and call it the 10 Commanders in Afghanistan, the Holy Bible from Israel by Net and Who? Till some real preacher took the microphone away.

Voicings of Fiery-Jeffrey: This is truly an undermining of the American flag, the laughing stock of the world, the 60 bucks a pop while religious heads and the Pope are considering excommunicating him, even though he's not Catholic. Man, oh Man, the stunts he'll pull off and has sold his Body and Soul to the Devil. I got my Gideons free. Did he bribe his passing of Sunday School?

Simple Snoopy Response to Fiery Jef in reply: Epstein (Jeffrey), you have never been up to any good! How you wish you'd thought of that idea earlier, right? You could even sell one Bible to yourself and keep the Prophet.

But your other business with chartered flights to the Island is really doing well, they say, and some are singing!

Countering Evil: The Closeness of the Church and State Separation Paradox

Anyhow, think of less perverted business ideas for Easter next year, which will not be on a Sunday. They are not going to keep that a Religious Secret and announce the day very late so that Biden does not proclaim Easter Sunday in 2025 again as the Transgender Day of Visibility. If anything, this is the first time ever that Baptists, Anarchists, Catholics, Hindus, and Muslims are all united on disguising the date of Easter, and moving it to a week day next year, to befuddle the already confused Joe, and mainly to preempt future Evil.

1. We hear that the Vatican is going to announce the date after the elections and not take a chance, and it will be a week day. To beat modern technology, AI, and surveillance, the Pope is Partnering with Native Americans and (Peoples of the First Nation– their name in

Canada), using smoke signal communications and signals, as both entities are adept in the ancient art of Smoke Signals. Actually, the Vatican is emulating something from the United States in using the language of the Navajo, a Native American tribe, to create an undecipherable code to hoodwink the very smart Japanese and Germans in World War II, something that they have never caught on.

We all do know that Joe is not smart enough to catch on to smoke technology because he thinks that the main reason for global warming is the Chiefs and Big Guys smoking their pipes on reservations, who, anyway, he also considers a threat to his power and glory! But it's the first-ever strategic and holy alliance of the Holy Spirit-inspired Vatican and Native Americans around one God, and a pantheon of gods and spirits. Tribe elders across North America have vowed to defeat this paleface elder at the Totem and electoral poles. He's now in a heap of trouble for speaking with a forked tongue, the dentures notwithstanding!

2. Secondly, the Vatican, wiser through experience, is still embittered by the persecution of Christians and the shambles Nero left the city of Rome in then, while he neglected official duties and fiddled, out of tune, never stopping. The Vatican is concerned that it's Yesterday Once More, with Nero, with Joe, is already letting the country burn with illegal immigration, inflation, and poverty if allowed any further woeful fiddling. They have decreed that Ole Cole Kaiser can call for his pipe, his wife, but fiddlers, in ones, twos, and threes, are off limits, fearful, he'd grab a fiddle from one and play.

    He's already got the persecution thing going; they have to stop him from fiddling and have called for additional security on rooftops to prevent him from going Up on the Roof to play! Some have argued that this is election interference by the Vatican, as his fiddling on land, air, and sea will raise funds for the party with people paying to stop screechy sounds, which sidekick does enough of anyways, with smiles.

3. Lastly, the Vatican has every reason to be pleased with the latest news in April 2024, for during the early years when it all started, Jesus said, "On This Rock, I Will Build My Church"? (Matthew 16). And now the "Rock" himself comes along, muscular and mountainous, a block of that Old Chip Peter, who was a boat and might action star in his own right, but nothing compared to the new deal, the Rock for the Ages, Gibraltar included.

    The Rock expressed some regret about his 2020 endorsement for Biden and Kamala Harris, saying he won't endorse any candidate this year. It's his affirmation of the rejection of failed policies that matters, not who he votes for. The Church should maintain its distance from the State, but the Rock saying this means, Good and Church are safe and "the gates of hell shall not prevail against it." All in all, it's just another rock in the wall for good change, and it will be good riddance to bad and the Hub and 'Axle of Evil' Snoopy says!

It is good to see that people are seeing through the failed misadventures of Sleepy.

Crossing Swords & At Loggerheads

Clearly, they say the Pope is pissed off with the Irish Catholic, Joe, and is prepared to break tradition and change the day of Easter next year to outfox Joe! Israel and its patriarchs, Abraham and Moses, are also unhappy in threatening that the US would be prepared to use its leverage to shape Israeli policy as a traitor to Israel, Schumer said recently in early April 2024.

By the way, Moses is more adept at using technology than Joe. You'll not find him getting mixed up with record players, remotes and other outdated gizmos. But Joe's from that bygone era. Now, as age and memory loss are debilitating, it is pitiful and embarrassing to see Joe struggle in public life. While we cut him some slack, for we truly love our Presidents, that decline is a part of the natural process of aging, and is best for nursing home and retired care, in private life, and not in running the country.

Moses, on the contrary, although ancient like Joe, is always his emphatic and confident self when it comes to laying down the law justly – pay heed DOJ! Moses, a pioneer in law, technology and communication, was the first to use a tablet. We're sure he'll fling his tablet at Joe because he's a prime candidate for anger management, and Apple and Samsung should be able to gladly offer a replacement, in case his original is out of warranty! We are referring to him shattering the Tablets of the Covenant (Exodus 32:19).

For that matter, even Jesus could do with some anger curtailment therapy, although he justifiably "overthrew the tables of the moneychangers," and the seats of them that sold doves, and said unto them, It is written, "My house shall be called the house of prayer, but ye have made it a den of thieves." Matthew 21:12-17 King James Version (KJV).

Upturning the Tables inside the Den of Thieves

Well, we certainly could do with his help in matters relating to overturning gaming tables in the dens of tramps and thieves (omitted gypsies, so they don't take offense, and cannot dishonor guitar virtuoso Django, and Mr. Fox though), even if it means the Son of God firing that ugly Son of a B for disobedience! For he said, Render unto Kaiser (and to Kinderella), what percentage is his, no messing around, no BS, or else!

Corporation, and the evil on earth, you just cannot go against men like Heston, who parted the Sea and Stilled the Waters, the latter to which Nightingale Anne from Canada, who concurred with in song, so beautifully!

Banished, but Welcome Back with Atonement for Sins

The rumor mill and audio from the grapevine (not from Marvin, though) revealed that the 'Smiling Irish Eyes' a powerful group in Ireland, and with diaspora members in every crevice and cranny on earth, after the Easter Sunday episode, have decided to disown all Irish links and relationships. They decided to banish and transfer this over to Wales, as Scotland rejected affiliation for two reasons:

1. The incompatibility of Kilts and "I got hairy legs that turned blonde in the sun." Those and other behaviors and comments were frowned upon, understandable for unwarranted exhibitionism and other reasons that we cannot mention here.

2. Freshly coming down the pike and off the airwaves, as the Joe case was being considered in Ireland, was the comment of veteran Democratic strategist James Carville of the party slump in polls, attributed to "too many preachy females" and "walking in on your grandma naked." They were aghast and stunned as their imaginations went into overdrive and they immediately visualized instead Grandpa Joe and a Kilt malfunction. It was an immediate rejection!

Luckily, for him, Wales conditionally accepted, but insisted that he'd be known as the Outlaw Joey Wales!

But the Irish are a truly forgiving lot as are all Americans, civilized and rude! They've said that after retirement, or rejection by voters in the United States in 2024, they'd welcome him back, with some genuine remorse, penance and atonement, as a Prodigal Irish Catholic Son!

We all love the younger Joe, but now the incline of running the country is out of step with the cognitive decline. Those baby steps on aircraft stairs and non-stick mats and handrails in the showers in the White House cannot go against the will of the man upstairs. Father time inevitably catches up! For some inexplicably, sooner than others, Joe!

Learned Lewis on Intellectual Property and Artist Rights under Copyright Laws

Continuing the Discourse with Fiery-Jeffrey: Perverted man, we know about your predatory escapades with "Body." My colleague, Learned Lewis, however, asked me to tell you, Epstein, to stop using the word "corrupt" with the phrase Body and Soul so irreverently to speak about politicians, as you are liable to be beaten up by his heroes, Coltrane, Satchmo, Hawkins, Green, Sarah, Ella, Sinatra, Bennett-Winehouse and many others.

Epstein, Lewis also advises - please be aware, that the composer of Body and Soul, Johnny Green in 1930, per Copyright laws, has 95 years for artistic copyright protection against any form of verbal and musical defilement. Green, therefore, has time till the next Presidential elections in 2028 worth of protection, as we believe that he and his publishers renewed the copyright for that timeless masterpiece at the end of the initial 28-year term! If not, Snoop and Learned are at their Beck and call to set the record straight!

Oh, speaking of Beck, how we miss Jeff Beck– he was inimitable, so he cannot be copied, no law needed, just recognition of his extraordinary talents! We know that someday we will earn those rights for our infinite wisdom as well– ha ha!

With the goodness of us, we *Pro Bono*, protect the work of all artists, and could have saved geniuses Page and Plant, Frey, and others precious time and money from idiocy and evil. We say this as we understand the law and its implications on infringement to copyright, from innuendo, lyrics, doublespeak, to music harmony in simple and extended forms, and will always smell a rat, if there are copycat(s) lurking somewhere and put an end to Evil!

As a sign of patriotism and a deep sense of gratitude to be living in this great country (now in tatters), proposals have been tendered to a) Making America Safe (will not add 'Again" as that is the copyright of President Donald Trump), in combatting Terrorism and b) In the Smartening of America. Federal Agencies, unfortunately, do not have listening posts and are missing Blueprints and Plans of geniuses! They have multiple mouths around their heads and two deaf ears, and so many excellent plans and proposals never see the light of day since bureaucracies and inflexibilities stifle innovation and creativity.

– End of the Legal Counsel on Copyrights and Things that Matter, by Learned Lewis.

While on my part, as a more sinfully Simple Snoopy in my taste, I am into contemporary music, from Taylor to Country, and an aficionado of hip hop, a proficient rapper myself, and with less leanings towards standards and the Classics. Will also tell Anita Baker to do so the same with regard to her Body and Soul and admonish your nastiness, Jeffrey!

Profile of Learned Lewis, is the studied, scholarly expert, less humble and equally blunt in his communication, but premises his responses carefully, with substantiation and draws from an infinite wealth of knowledge to base his rationale. Literature, law, science, music, and multi-disciplinary knowledge are invoked by both journalists; however, the inevitable conclusion is also the title of this Book, which the reader and a great part of America may agree once this book is read.

An Example of Learned Lewis at Work:

Countering the Guillotine & Bastille Mob: Several of the mob belonging to this category showed up to heap praise for the prosecutions against Donald Trump and, when asked to explain, turned hostile. The Bastille Mob refers to the analogy of the mentality of incitement and rush to be judge, jury, and executioner, as was on that fateful day in Paris, France, on 14 July 1789, which subsequently led to the French Revolution. That same mob mentality pervades in respect of former president Donald Trump, as hordes are blinded by party affiliation, and there is imperviousness to legal reasoning and little to no understanding of the basic requirement of law and justice, to a fair trial, due process, and human decency, with the desire for summary execution.

Summed up, the **Guillotine & Bastille Mob** comments were: Trump all day for crime, prison inmate president, or most indictments, and these are but just a few of nasty charges believed to be true– and their rush to judgment.

Learned Lewis Response: There's a similar or greater chance, statistically speaking, of you going to prison than Donald Trump. Better watch it! No wife beating, adultery, road rage, thieving thy neighbor's wife or goods, because there are cameras everywhere and they'll catch and arrest ya! Keep it clean and stay away from trouble in short.

That stunned the morons! They had never heard anything like this nor expected it.

Our Advice for Guillotine & Bastille Mob Reformation:

Think Twice, Be Nice!

To Their Great Pretender Pretense on a Platter Act:

Feign all Sugar and Spice at Face Value, but

Back Stab and Deny before the Rooster Crows Thrice!

Explanation by LL: President Trump has not been convicted of any crimes! Those phony indictments will be tossed out on appeal, one by one! Tainted juries, weaponized judges, and politically prejudiced prosecutors will indict a ham and toads like you (and me – by the idea of fairness to get them to see the idiocy of foolishness). I will explain further to you.

An indictment, by definition, is the formal, legal accusation of a crime against a person by the state prosecutor, DA, (the executive power, etc., depending on the level of government). A conviction, on the other hand, is a ruling or judgment from the judicial branch of the state via the state's judicial branch, requiring irrefutably that the indictment is supported by evidence, beyond a reasonable doubt.

Handling the Rabid Guillotine & Bastille Mob without CDC/Fauci's Assistance:

Is that a joke? A mob member screamed in the wind (as loud as it did for Jimi and "Mary"). I'd say, someone with 88 charges in 4 different jurisdictions is sure to be convicted of something with prison time. Since you know nothing about me, you are concocting the information to make a prediction. But I know me, I know the law, and I have read the indictments.

Trump has a 100+ times more chance than I do. But thanks for the made-up shit math. So, the probability of going to prison is higher for a random person who has never been charged with a crime and who does not engage in criminal activity, vs. the 0RANGE D0UCH who has been charged with 88 felonies in 4 different jurisdictions. Must be new MAGA-math.

Learned Lewis: No joke- enroll in my class and I will teach you law, statistics, and more, even if math challenged will dum and dummer it down for ya!

Probability means, the random and equal chance of some occurrence of something or event, to anyone selected from the population. I do not need to know anyone to make a prediction. It's a level playing field, and randomly selecting from names from a hat, with a blindfold on– your name in that hat means you could be picked from that hat and say that you could go to prison. Stay away from trouble, and keep it honest and clean!

The probability and equal likelihood of 'conviction' of a crime for anyone and you and DT, thus, would be the same, as you may be charged with wife beating, molesting, etc. By that time, from now to conviction in the future, before November 2024. That probability of being imprisoned, hence, remains the same. Whatever your orange or chameleonic color is, it does not matter! That probability remains the same for him, you, or and anyone– got it?

Higher the Ignorance of Law Fundamentals, the Greater the Hate Vitriol

The indictments are not final, just like Biden's innocence or guilt. What is your level of education, by the way? Law and Statistics seem way above your dimwitted understanding. Those indictments are worthless by a tainted set up and they will be thrown out. Therefore, the probability remains equal of you going to prison, as anyone else randomly selected from the population.

Aside from statistics, you seem to severely lack understanding of the fundamentals of law on which our system of justice is supposedly founded. That is the presumption of innocence, the rule of law and justice, and the unbiased and equal application of the law. Acquire this knowledge, complete high school, begin college, study for the LSAT, and send me your essay for admission to law school to determine if the knowledge of critical thinking and suitability to understand legal precepts, jurisprudence, and the finer aspects are there. If successful, I will award tuition tuition-free scholarships for the entire degree. Till then, it will be continued exposure of one-sided ignorance, which cannot be bliss.

I also want you to be aware of the other side of statistics, as Disraeli said, 'There are three kinds of lies: lies, damned lies, and statistics', and Mark Twain said, 'Get your facts first, and then you can distort them as much as you please. (Facts are stubborn, but statistics are more pliable).

What I mean is that understanding the weaponization of the system by the elderly man with a fading memory has evil imprinted.

The Guillotine & Bastille Mob: Well, we've had fun discussing. The conversations, although ugly, have yielded food for thought.

Learned Lewis: I thought to myself, mission accomplished, had sown the seeds of doubt and introduced the need for a holistic look at facts. There is time for them to ponder! Whew, after I went at it hammer and tongs, I felt like had earned a well-deserved rest, not unlike Henry Wadsworth Longfellow's The Village Blacksmith:

> Each morning sees some task begin,
>
> Each evening sees it close;
>
> Something attempted, something done,
>
> Has earned a night's repose.

Setting the Stage for Probing Mayhem - Journalistic Stylings in Variance

Having introduced the two investigative journalists, it will be best for them to take over and convey their findings and story with no reservations, as they always do. In these investigations, I was informed, they started politically independent, neutral, and as fence-sitters, but seeing how the vilified Donald Trump was "Outnumbered" in the liberal media, where they operated, they gravitated towards the underdog for his better vision for America.

From here on, it is the narrative and voice of Simple Snoopy you will hear, and calling upon the astute Learned Lewis when needed.

Chapter 2:
Welcome Change with Trump for a New Tomorrow!

Learned Lewis and Simple Snoopy give thanks to the God of Good over Satanic Evil, that the floor is ours now with that fine introduction.

From the exhaustive research that will unfold, we defy the conventional and sometimes proceed in reverse gear. From the research findings, analysis and conclusions, we would like to convey the optimism of **Change with Trump for a New Tomorrow.**

As the first preparing for positive and welcome change after a disastrous four years, soon to be gone by, will be the dawn of a new era, of prosperity and safety. America has the talent, and our people must be empowered with good business and policy strategies to succeed. As a nation, we all know, this is the reason for leading the world. That advantage is being surrendered by unintelligent and ill-advised strategies and leadership.

The considerable skills and knowledge that reside in us are from the immense capabilities of our people, with the abundant blessings as One Nation unto God! It is time to forge ahead for prosperity and better times and consider the failed policies of Biden as one vivid nightmare that we should awaken from and resolve to end. It is time to elevate our standard of life and living.

Unprecedented Political Vengeance Driven Adversity

Adversity is always assured (they'll come after you) for those who want to challenge the establishment; now it's called the Old Boys Club, which we think is a fit that Cochrane would say Yes, Perfecto! For they (Ole and Co.) want to rule unhindered and in perpetuity, while true in any walk of life. In politics, it means ruling the roost and preventing some from the emerging talent pool from making it, while the glass ceiling and other barriers also make it difficult for the talented and aspiring, but may be shut out with smiles, any which way?

In politics, grizzled veterans jostle for power, as the old guard holds on to it, often precariously. The political immaturity and the tendencies of the uninitiated and not fully versed in the cut-throat nature of the business often succumb and see their political promise, from the early promise, fade and plummet to the abyss of the forgotten. Many self-centered (most are) career politicians, over time, and have only incessantly corroborated the George Bernard Shaw notion of the profession being the last resort of the scoundrel.

Trump's Continuous Triumph over Adversity

This book is about Trump's continuous triumph over adversity, about the remarkable saga of how one man, Donald Trump, facing the most profound vilification possibly in the history of mankind, maintains not only his sanity but shows a good and clean heart for America. He has continued to prevail and eventually should overcome unprecedented disdain and hate in the form of prosecutions, lawsuits and other spiteful manifestations of extreme weaponization that has made countless new followers and fans in the country, including minorities, to all others.

The remarkable loyalty of those who stand by him should be acknowledged and praised as well, whether intellectuals to blue-collar and everyday citizens of America, the magnificent. This book is not about the glorification of one man. It is about critical thinking and seeing the tremendous one-sided fight, which led to the support of the underdog, having experienced that from the vantage point of disadvantaged and privileged all but too often, living in America.

Simple Snoopy: Donald Trump has been called a Russian agent, Rasputin, and some of the most horrible names imaginable, from the exalted messiah to the meanest, cheat, thief, thug, rapist, etc., all out of political hate, by the nobody's and bigwigs, and but principally stemming from sheer envy of his brashness, business acumen, and his mega political success. The man epitomizes bravery, defies conventional political cunning, and is for people and country.

But, try as hard as you may – You Cannot Keep a Good Man Down! And the world and Many Americans Want Donald Trump to arrest the decline! So, join the club, the movement of truth, and "Don't let them fool ya, or even try to school ya, oh no," as the revered Rastafarian poet Bob Marley would say.

The name calling of Donald Trump has been mild in contrast to the other candidates: Sleepy Joe, the Big Guy, Mr. 10%, etc., and even criminality timid in sentences, rather more in sympathy and showing respect for his age, at his fumbles, gaffes, stumbles, and exponentially worsening cognitive declines – he is falling apart each day. We've surely never seen anything as dramatic as this also in the history of mankind!

Man, and God forbid, if anything were to happen to him, Ms. Giggly would be the default President. She's the hardest praying person in America for the last few years they say. I've heard she goes down on bended knees each night to pray and ask so that she Receives and is bestowed the title. She doesn't want it to be her dream, but it is coming true, from the California bussing days of old, which lacked soul. The Presidency, by default, would be simply terrible – I'm sure you will agree for someone so undeserving!

Psychology Strategy and Imparting Quality Education

Now, let me give you a sneak preview of my style. It can be termed 'Both Sides Now' journalistic, investigative psychology intended to probe the minds of those I am speaking with. My aim, as stated, is to uncover knowledge deficits and open minds so that the individual or group can mull things over and be informed. We want an intelligent Electorate in the United States in November 2024, and strive for achieving that possibility, as may be within our capabilities.

So first, when encountering a hostile and partisan individual or group, I may lower their defenses by stroking their egos and making them feel enormous. Often, calling them world-famous figures at times may help, but it is one of many different ways. We play it by ear and use legal notes and common-sense skills for the takedowns to educate on the truth. The genuineness in accepting valid arguments on both sides of the aisle helps to instill the confidence to 'spill the beans' of hate or love. Thereafter, they are ripe to give respect to or tear apart if there is ignorance in arguments, with effective rebuttals – nothing personal ever! All in good humor, which is excellent for ridicule and dissemination of education on law, etc.

Perhaps I should explain. Here is just the gist, minus the legal lectures on the equal application of the law and more:

Maybe pure imagination, but I have seen the actor Eastwood show up and a variety of other big names. This Eastwood. Instantly, after calling the guy that name, I surmise, imagined himself to be the action hero, with that shawl draped on, the six guns drawn and blazing, and that cigar in the corner of his mouth, and that drawl begins, but the problem with the inflated ego, is the nonsense spewing. A Pam or Pamela, also made a presence and was inspired to rant hate, simply because I mistook her for Anderson, and same story, the imagination of being the star of Baywatch took over. Allow me to elucidate:

King Clint: Nothing changes the fact that Trump broke the law (referring to January 6).

Simple Snoopy: Wow Eastwood, it's ok to Hang 'em High then? Just get 'em and string 'em up then, eh? Quick justice, a fake trial, and get it over with - Just follow the orders and do anything to get him! – the rapid-fire hate continued by the Hero against the villain (Trump), with a slew of expletives, that I am tempted to quote, but will refrain from doing so, in good taste!

Eastwood, so you are saying it's The Law of the Lariat or Lawless, eh? Not examining how those charges were framed, their merits, nothing! Broke the law according to whom?

In a close election, it is normal to investigate and see where and if there were missed counts, human errors, and so forth. Gore did it during the Hanging Chads days, and it was not considered illegal but a process of verification. For him, luckily, the President's job did not transpire, and remuneratively, it would be peanuts compared to the raking in of millions from making every day a greater scare than the one day of the scariest Halloween sounds imaginable, with the global warming scamming he perpetuates.

Of course, no two situations are ever the same, but nevertheless, they have a different set of standards and lenses – motive – Perpetuity in Power. "Political power grows out of the barrel of a gun," famously said by Chinese Communist leader Mao Zedong. Millions of Americans now propose that power and weaponization come from the unequal and biased application of the law by the weaponized DOJ, as also believed by one of the greatest political families in the United States, RFK, Jr. You'd better watch your tongue gun totin, Eastwood.

For your Information, in March 2024, human error was found in the Chicago Board of Elections, and the explanation of why more than 10,000 ballots did not get included and caused errors and unofficial counts lower than projected.

This seems more likely orchestrated from higher up, and these puppets on a string are manipulated in Georgia. Will the White House logs on visitor visits by Willis, perhaps Wade as well, in accompaniment, transcripts, and emails reveal sinister evil emanating from the very top? Let's give peace a chance man, and not be rabid here, agree, or we agree to disagree? Think it over!

Note by Note, from Learned Lewis: Let's clarify that this was the fake Eastwood and not the beloved American actor and filmmaker Clint Eastwood, whose many accomplishments and versatility include, in addition to being an accomplished pianist and composer, even writing for the pretty pianist Diana Krall.

The God of Movies and of Guitar, well, there are commonalities, noted our expert, who **LL,** who makes the most unusual correlations, the mark of a true genius: Clint Eastwood fondness for the Errol Garner jazz standard "Misty" is well known, while Jimi Hendrix could play in Eb, the original key, which may account for his innate sense of musical harmony and jazz voicings evident in his subtle and not overly-stated phrasings, depicted the ear for extended harmony. In his playing. Learned Lewis admits quite gracefully that he has neither the looks of Eastwood nor the "Fire" of Jimi in his Pianistic and Guitar excursions.

Layla Nordstrom and Stonehenge (a two-some vile duo): Yelled on hearing the above: What planet did you come in from, must not have had radio contact. You're from the corrupt world of MAGA.

Simple Snoopy: Layla -I'm not from your corrupt world – the view of mine is for your education, on the Federal Election Commission, the rule of law, freedom of speech, and jurisprudential principles of equal justice for all, etc.

True, I gave up radio a long time ago - have Internet now. Are you still living in Radio Ga-Ga Days, and it appears you are from the Daft Side of the Moon? Layla, we're beggin' you to see the truth, and you are getting no one to their knees. Layla, Errata: One thing I do know, is that you and StoneHead prevent you from understanding the law because hatred is in there from geological ages.

Let's fathom if there is any corruption in High Places. The courts should ask them to explain-clearly - that party loyalty is obfuscating dense-stoned-brains.

The Extensive Travels of Simple Snoopy and Learned Lewis

Using deep analysis, multi-disciplinary knowledge of law, management, education, and uncommon common sense, investigative journalists. Simple Snoopy and Learned Lewis engage in discourse with audiences, aka, at times, debating, arguing, influencing, and where possibly inspiring. The educationist perspective in the personal endeavor is to convince supporters and adversaries that there are two sides to every story, and knowing both sides is useful to increase one's awareness of life, the vagaries of and knowledge in its limitless forms.

The aim of these discussions and discourse is to lower the hate and heat and heal. In the process, draw from existing knowledge, using humor, repartee, and drawing from literature, music, and any and all forms of persuasion to coax and open minds to see "Both Sides Now." If insulted, respond in kind, and if ridiculed, take the high road (when possible) and use education to again show the logic and the imperatives of a holistic review of facts and fiction.

Our foray into public forums revealed that this is largely dominated by the entrenched liberal idealists. While we are neutral and strive to provoke both sides (and the unsure/undecided) of the political divide, we, unfortunately, found one side more predominant, with the tendency to shut down the conservative side and all other voices of reason or dissent. That presented unique challenges. However, the skilled debaters we are, nothing has proved insurmountable to explain, counter, or just instill a message of reason and common sense, favoring the need for patience and the truth.

The appellate process must rectify inequities, if any. Give them time and stop cursing if they deliberate. Justice delayed is justice that is weighed and deliberated upon carefully.

Gutsy, Intelligent, and Sincere

The Bravest Man in America is undoubtedly former President Donald Trump. Lesser mortals would easily buckle and fold under such relentless vilification and quell such a voice into silence and submission. President Donald Trump would even consider (April 7, 2024) it to be his "great honor" to go to jail, be the US version of Nelson Mandela, and fight for freedom of speech on the charges levied on what is known as the hush-money payment to a porn star.

Trump, while visibly since 2020, a little older, like all of us, the wisdom and coherence are undiminished in his form and style of articulation, which comes from what is inborn – business leadership that is avowedly for America! That shouldn't change, for he is a showman, a good businessman, and a compassionate human being who speaks his mind straight from his heart. Now, all that will be argued and debated, with good intention by us and otherwise by many.

I am sure that if you open almost any page in this book, and you will find legal imperatives, mirth, humor, and sadness as well at times, but that's life as well! In the end, while democracy is seemingly in shambles in the USA, the same vile kind of games seem to be happening elsewhere. Those countries introspectively would know themselves. However, when it's all said and done, the American people are the finest in the world.

We need to just cast aside all forms of inequality on the political divide and allow Americans to not be forced to squabble and quarrel because of the evil politics does to incite and inflame dissent.

Oh, those Politicians! Some are simply bigger scoundrels than others – my apologies to George Bernard Shaw for a little distortion of his famous words! I think that the quote 'Patriotism is the last refuge for a scoundrel,' from Dr. Samuel Johnson also applies to all the insurrection nonsense for a riot gone awry on January 6, despite the calls for help to have measures in place, informing those in charge, and the word "peacefully" deliberately ignored.

Start Spreadin' The Real News

One news caption read: Trump should be barred from blaming others for Jan. 6. Learned Lewis, a regular debater, schooled and steeped in-laws and management countered: Precisely: "Trump should be barred from blaming others" - He should only blame the Special Counsel and 4 fingers are pointing back at him for

1) Never mentioning **"peacefully."**

2) The origins of the weaponization of the Judicial System.

3) Politicization and Election Interference.

4) A blatant Fit to Convict Scheming.

How can anyone not see that January 6 was a mob caught up in the moment in a frenzy, as in any riotous event, and here emotions were running high? Quit this political persecution and vilification. Its persecution mania on party lines with the pretense of acting for the cause of justice, is terribly distressing and violates the fundamental tenets of equality for all unto the law.

Insurrection is made-up hype. Let's see the finer aspects of it here:

It is also untrue, according to the law. Seditious conspiracy is US code 2384, and Insurrection/Rebellion is US code 2383 – read these up, for no one has been charged with these crimes. Wrong is every gullible hater who believes that to be true, only for argument's sake, but knows in their hearts it was just on the spur-of-the-moment what became an out-of-control mob and not orchestrated, and any call of insurrection is an insult to the intelligence of Americans.

Learned Lewis, horrorstruck and dismayed at the lack of knowledge, said, "Why can't people understand and deliberately air ignorance? Schooling has never been more accessible through the asynchronous capabilities of online learning as education is now not constrained by geography, age, and other barriers. We are indeed on the cusp of an educational revolution, as computers have become cheaper, learners are older as age is no bar, and the knowledge available at one's fingertips is unquantifiable, yet stupidity can persist."

The simple truth is that those who fail to move with the tide may be left behind while the world moves ahead, and Bad Bidenomics and illegal immigration are not a solution. These are two of the major problems and a burden brought upon us by this antiquated human being.

America, I suggest that we stop using the word **'Witch-Hunt,'** in describing the persecution of former President Donald Trump! It is just too mild and overly dependent on the broom, potions, and spells. Moreover, we also have Wendy the Good Little Witch, and it would be terrible to link her and good and bad witches to Evil, barring Smiley, of course. What we are talking about here is the **Evil King of Kingly Kings** ever to rule over Man and Womankind!

In an Unequal World, the Oppressed Always Overcome Evil!

The never-ending inequality is distressing, whether it is political persuasion, gender and sexual orientation, race, age, or whatever else. But the confidence in one's God-given talent, and that built and acquired with diligence, should be enough to rise above the crowd and shame those who unsuccessfully place hurdles in the quest and path of success.

For all its vaunted proclamations of civil justice and fairness, the results and realities of equal opportunity generally speak otherwise. It is resourceful and diligent, and those who strive to excel will find that success is there with authentic intent and prudent audaciousness. This intent to do good for America is explicit in Trump and Biden. However, the latter needs to rethink many things. Let's see some hard-hitting trading of insults, innuendo, and spirited and mean conversations. No holds barred. The games begin and continue as we share our experiences.

The issues are well known of weaponization, illegal immigration trumped up charges of Caroll in Wonderland-Roxanne and Flaunty-Jaunty Daniels in a Storm (several in our discussions cleverly called both 'hoes' and 'hose" on social media, for obvious reasons, needing no explanation on strategies to beat) and all the current and ongoing mayhem and vitriol, as they occurred, and continue. There is no sequence, chronology and no order, as the common thread is weaponization. Moreover, nothing is seemingly logical about the one-sided attacks.

Chapter 3:
Musings I: From the Desks of Learned Lewis and Simple Snoopy

We are so tired of seeing Americans make no progress over the last few years with the disastrous policies of Biden. Look at how Trump is handling the lawsuits, raising money to counter the ridiculous bonds, even scaled it down to 177 million, and then is simultaneously countering the predators - lingerie trying out Carroll-Roxanne and so-called hush-up for porn star, Flaunty-Jaunty Daniels.

Trump has been succeeding one step and one day at a time. Guess what, no matter what your religious or other belief, his prayer is perhaps: One day at a time, sweet Jesus, Thats all I'm asking of You. Just give me the strength to do every day what I have to do!

Simple Snoopy: From religious to the perverse, I'd simply say to them Foxy Ladies. From what name calling I saw on social media, it was often: **Hoe, Hoe, Hoe.** Like Santa said, you are not going to get no big gifts! Need water **Hose, Hose, Hose,** to douse the miscalculations of the hallucinations and building castles in the air!

While I was not so straightforward and tried to disguise, using 'hoe,' Mr. Sudbury wasn't and was brutally honest on 18 Apr 2024.

A Biden diehard said: I am not supporting Trump, but you have to admire the virility though of Trump! He's got women chasin' after him! You'd possibly only have your old one naggin' ya! The last stud in the White House was Bill from our party.

Mr. Sudbury: whores all its money no other reason, set up to go after Trump! The formula is simple and not surprising:

To bring a good man down, you use an evil woman! Eve, Delilah, Lady Macbeth! Now E. Carroll and Stormy Daniels.

Character Assassination of Trump Not Working:

The world sees how he has been deliberately weighed down to prevent him from contesting the collections, but we Americans of every race, creed, and color see the ultimate aim in weaponization. Nevertheless, we see Trump emerging victorious, which is an inspiration for all of us - his resoluteness and bravery, and really all to serve America.

Despite the façade of outward calmness in his demeanor, we know that what Donald Trump has been put through since 2016 would devastate lesser mortals, yet he plows on undeterred and despite the internal turmoil. For that, we call him **the Bravest Man in the World and America!**

Trump Always Shows Up! Present Where Most Needed

Trump has got the smarts to lead again, believes in growth and diversification for America, to reclaim our status in energy, manufacturing and other areas squandered by the policies of career Joe, who's too weak and needs two former guys to prop him up and bail him out of messes in real time and behind the scenes. The effort to raise monies for the election in ritzy-glitzy fundraising, are comical, moderated by late-night talk show host Stephen Colbert. It was like the blundering Three Stooges, minus the laughs, artificial, and contrived, unlike those lovable legends.

A mere few miles away, Donald Trump was paying tribute to an American life and a true hero. We can see who is truly for America, and vested interests! New York City Police Officer Jonathan Diller at a Massapequa Park, Long Island funeral home, some 40 miles from Manhattan.

Hey, ex-Presidents, is the situation so bad? You were elected, served, and served your terms. Now, this is not **'Extended Stay America!'** Men of your stature and wisdom should know that partaking in active politics means you are also engaged in election subversion for the weak candidate, and hanging on only diminishes your legacies. Get off the scene, man, and let new and younger talent emerge. With you and your wives vying for office, it is a duplicitous attempt to make the office of the President a dynasty.

What a disgrace that two of you show up amidst all the fanfare and the few wisecracks, don't impress sensible and everyday Americans at all. When people are not better off, which one of you also said in no uncertain terms, with some cover up, which fell flat. You are going against America and the Truth! The country is in a mess; stop Play Acting.

Lamentable Dereliction of Duty: Tired & Clueless Leadership

If you couldn't show up for the wake of the fallen officer, couldn't you have observed a minute's silence for an American killed in the line of duty? It is these little things that matter to Americans, not raking in those $25 + million dollars. But then again, the cops are always thought of rather poorly; it appears by the party folks, even though they give so much to the country and their selfless dedication and devotion to serving us, is often with risk to their lives, as did Police Officer Jason Diller.

Have you ever voiced your opinions on law and order, the safety of Americans, preserving our borders, and the cost of living and our standards? Or is it just those free trade deals that still persist and you are enamored with, which have only made other countries richer and turned several of our cities into ghost towns

The Lack of Confidence in Joe by ex-Presidents Obama and Clinton

America will surely see the telltale signs of the lack of confidence by ex-Presidents Clinton and Obama, at the lavish fundraiser in March 2024. A foreboding sense of despair here, that all Americans will realize, is that they recognize it has been a job poorly done, from their words at the Pomp and Circumstance event at Radio Hall in New York City:

1. Praise where it is due, which Clinton rightly did in his later damage control for reasoning that it was an economy built by Democrats, is pure nonsense and just an example of the slick and customary doublespeak he's known for: "President **Trump, let's be honest, had a pretty good couple of years** because he stole them from Barack Obama."

2. Clinton added. "Well, what happened was actually job growth under President Trump was slower than it was under President Obama and Biden. But people didn't feel it. It takes a while to feel it." **Learned Lewis** replying: The vast majority in the nation believes that the times under President Trump's term were far better for the home, at the pump, and to the wallet, Mister Slickster! Groceries were heapa cheapa, so was gas, and buying a home. It's called consumer confidence reflective in our economic indicators, and now the misery and crying soul of America for better days with Let Down! The ground realities speak the horrors, and not all that fallacious mumbo-jumbo of the Stock Exchange.

3. But the Icing on the cake, and the admittance that times were better earlier, is here: "If you're working hard, and your paycheck is getting stretched beyond the breaking point, and you're worried about rent, and you're concerned about the price of gas, it's understandable," Obama said. Wow, Mr. President, we admire your honesty, and it's akin to reconciling that the unsinkable Titanic in Joe has hit Icebergs, and the inevitable and the distress signals are rather late.

   You, Sirs, have shown up for your colleague, and the contrived humor belies the true concerns, in your words, which are those of true American leaders, we revere and admire. For despite all the little and major differences we may have, Presidents Clinton, Bush, Obama, Trump, and Biden, are the pride of America! You have, by showing up for a money-making event, not earned what Aretha said, our profound 'RESPECT.'

You distinguished Sirs, cannot color the harsh hardships everyday American face. We know our adeptness for glibness, cover-ups, and apologies. The real picture shows the economy is bad – your side-tracking economic reality of who inherited a strong economy from whom is duplicitous, insincere, and awkwardly dishonest because you, in your own heart and mind, know you are not speaking the truth!

President Obama, you couldn't have said it better, "Don't underestimate Joe Biden's ability to F-things up." He's done just that in the last 4 years!

With a heavy heart, and it is a great moment of shame that here we, humble journalists, find ourselves lecturing to the greatest men on earth. But what choice do we have? For the Sky is Crying, economic hardship from the Streets of Philadelphia, to all of America. I'm sure we will meet soon in better times, as All (Bad) Things Must pass, as George said, and I tip my hat to the real Elmo (James), Bruce as well. America is too precious to be the victim of bad policies, from which we will not likely recover, or as John said, 'Let's give peace (and prosperity, if I may add) a chance with better times for the incredible USA!'

What! Chants of Death to America now on April 15, 2024? This is what your policies have done, Joe. This is the real insurrection and sedition! This would never happen under a Donald Trump presidency! The people of America will vote for change this time!

Let's look at the declining cognitive side of things – America, the Greatest Nation on Earth, cannot have and stumbling, fumbling, and declining guy whose sole motivation to contest now and continuance will be to mitigate, cover up, and do personal damage control, not for the real purpose to lead the country to a thriving and prosperous future.

Served Well, Now We're Beggin' Ya to Depart the Building.

While those two ex-Presidents should have left the building, not to return a long time ago, they linger only to stay relevant, like prize fighters past the pink of their prime! We'd think they are all shook up with the mess as well. They are from, or in their prime before and during, the Floyd era and may well say that Joe is comfortably dumb and, therefore, must do something (besides Layla) to help ease his troubled, dazed, and confused mind, and we'd get Jagger to sing Time is On Your Side, no, it's not!

We recommend lowering risks, and really that no one wants to have 'all eggs in one basket,' and going after Electric and abandoning traditional is foolish and uneducated. Today, most businesses, where possible, are eager to diversify, explore test the waters before taking radical steps and decisions to "phase out" fossil fuels. Man, he's got environment in the brain and pressure by the few nasty skirts in the party, called the Vile Squad.

Do not eliminate, as uneducated, any form of technology and resource Politician man when you do not know enough about science. Provoke parallel innovation in what exists and in the new, for example, oil companies investing in green and alternative sources of renewable while also allocating investments for research aimed at improving and reducing carbon emissions of fossil fuels.

Stimulate incremental and astute diversification, and allow current and future technologies to exist and evolve without "phasing" out nonsense you spewed, trying to show off! Let the fittest survive like Darwin said, (pertinent to you as well) rather than elimination or forced cannibalization of energy sources and technology.

It is important for policymakers to be acquainted with the realities of today and the future. We should play to our known strengths, shore up our limitations, and function within the constraints of our financial capabilities and resources. Do things after a studied approach to examine the opportunities, the challenges, and the pitfalls, and not rush blindly into shutting town pipelines, allowing crime to flourish unchecked and with poor policies, for these are all related to the happiness of Americans.

The key to current and renewable sources of energy may be at all times to closely scan, monitor, and evaluate different scenarios, using 'what if' simulations of the consequences and fallouts, etc., before momentous decisions are made that are not on a whim and a fancy, personal ignorance, and the pressures of the Green and Socialist radicals in the party.

The Truth Man: A Wonderful Country in Despair – Look What You've Done!

The $25 Million you made in Radio City Music Hall on Thursday, March 20, 2024, was drowned out by the protests to a large extent, but more so by the show acting of the ex-presidents of support to the party. The words of the past two are a clear indication Joe is in trouble with poor support within, and here's the most gut-wrenching one from a retired gentleman that could not have been said better, which is truly the state of the country:

"People keep quoting NASDAQ and all of the other stocks or markets that have gone up significantly. Again, these do not represent the gas pump or prices at the market. We are average senior Americans. We have no pensions; I work a part-time job, and we are OK. But it isn't getting any easier, and all the talk about how good things are doesn't explain the can of corn that used to cost sixty cents three years ago is now a dollar eighty-two."

Trump, in his next term, must learn to maintain and bring back his progressive policies. He must show a continued appreciation for measured risk and innovation, focus on the wealth creation of the USA, and provide the impetus to foster innovation; this is Snoop and learned signing off with these musings for now.

Chapter 4:
Who is Behind it All and What Are the Solutions?

Whoever is behind it all would need a patient look at things after to 2024 election. Leading the charge may be President Joe Biden; we will need to see. However, in his contemptuous mocking of Donald Trump's persecution imposed financial woes, at a recent campaign event in Texas, he seemed rather pleased: "Just the other day, a defeated-looking man came up to me and said, 'Mr. President, I have crushing debt, and I'm completely wiped out,'" Biden said. "And I had to look at him and say, 'Donald, I'm sorry. I can't help you."

Trump, in that week filed a statement in court saying he's been rejected by 30 companies as he seeks to pay off his $464 million bond from his fraud case. New York Attorney General Letitia James' viciousness was on undiluted display, with the public boasts of being already moving to seize his assets if he was unable to pay by Monday's (March 25, 2024) deadline. Is this the permissible conduct of an official? No, it is not! The behavior is for career and fame, but what you'll get is a shame, justly deserved for playing around with justice!

The "Trump" said he had nearly $500M in cash, suggested he could afford bond in the New York AG case, and slammed the 'hack' judge – the world agreed on the persecution.

Response to Lady Alright: As an independent, I'd club you with the fraud-perpetuating hate of the Guillotine and Bastille mob, duped by their duplicity and hate indoctrination for the other political party. Will urge all to get a deeper understanding of the rule of law, due process, the presumption of innocence, the equal application of law and justice, and true democratic traditions; we seem to be losing it.

Whether he pays or not, you and I are not going to get a dime for the limited value in useless conjecture and taking pleasure in the difficulties of others! Keep your own house in order, and save yourself from the vicious cycle of perpetual credit card debt. Don't you see the plight of most Americans, Ma'am Madeline?

Getting to the Bottom of Who's Leading this Weaponization

Again, America wants to know who is behind all this political vindictiveness and vengeance. It is only the extraordinarily strong-willed and determined Donald Trump who has to wage fierce legal battles against those who go after him with impunity. The clear motive is to handcuff him with legal cases and financial constraints to prevent him from dedicating time to the campaign. America is not taking kindly to holding him back, and many have vowed that this form of weaponization will be decided at the ballot.

We say that this should never ever happen again and posit that this requires a radical review and transformation of established principles, doctrines, and even lyrics that were fine for gentlemanliness of the past and not the unprecedented evil that has been thrust upon us by Joe –

Increasing in age, but the Evil has always been there, Americans say! **Undoubtedly, the bBravest man on the Planet is Donald Trump.**

Solution One:

New York, New York, Changing the Tune, Amending the Lyrics!

The New York Business state of mind is one of depression. Start spreading the news of the inevitability of businesses leavin' today or tomorrow and want to be no part of it! A demented judge lacking real-estate and business knowledge and an evil prosecutor who found Trump guilty even before the commencement of investigations have eroded the confidence of businesses in the country and worldwide.

We'll ask **Jon-Bon** to sing from across the Hudson – You Give Justice a Bad Name! No guarantee he'd oblige. We hope our findings make Americans of star power and otherwise see what is going on and vote intelligently and confidentially, so their choice is never known – evil can be dangerous as well to America.

The image of New York City as the financial district and capital of the world has suffered irreparable damage thanks to idiots Alvin Chipmunk, Ergonomic, and Donor Marchant. But again, the common theme in all this points to the ruses, ploys, and tricks of the authoritative evil at the helm. The consequence of the combo of evil and ignorance has played havoc with a) energy, which had repercussions on the increase in gas and food prices overall, and b) pains in the electric vehicle industry, with pressures on the industry, falling under the spell of climate and green alarmists, with knowledge inadequacies in an unproven cause of global warming c) chaos in law and order, and women and Asians getting punched in the face, and the pressures of immigration on the city to house them.

Mr. Wonderful O'Leary, the Canadian businessman, investor, journalist, and television personality, called this terror in New York on Trump, rightly, an 'extraordinary assault' on the American brand, reprehensible and unfair to businesses, investors, and investments. We agree that the message to investors in the most powerful country is that they should think twice about doing business in New York or America.

Solution Two:

Judicial Process Reengineering (JPR)

Learned Lewis is possibly going to render a recommendation that may be as ground-breaking and momentous (**Snoopy:** I'd take this with a grain of salt, but you never know, the man has a heap of wisdom that I can brag about, which I wouldn't be able to with that chipmunk Alvin) as the decision on a cold December in 1801, in one of the most famous cases in the history of the United States in Marbury v. Madison (1803).

Learned Lewis: We leave reviewing the case in its entirety to you, as it would make the reader appreciate the wisdom of the courts and judicial precedence that set the course of an important principle of law in the United States and around the world. However, here, just a short synopsis is possible.

The Facts, Stated with No Lies – Snoopy, Not Involved: The President in 1801 was John Adams. At the end of his term in 1801, President Adams issued William Marbury a commission as justice of the peace, which the incoming and new Secretary of State, James Madison, refused to deliver to him. The ensuing confrontation saw Marbury sue to obtain the commission. The profound declaration by the then Chief Justice John Marshall was that "a law repugnant to the Constitution is void."

Thus, in the landmark decision of Marshall in Marbury v. Madison, Chief Justice John Marshall emphatically laid the principle of judicial review as the foundational cornerstone with respect to the oversight measures to buttress the system of "checks and balances." In lay terms, this was intended to 'clip the wings' vested in the otherwise arbitrary powers of the Federal Government and thereby prevent any one branch of the Federal Government from becoming too powerful – aka, too big for its boots.

The Supreme Court was empowered with the power to declare unconstitutional, a law although passed by Congress and signed by the President, although the Constitution itself did not provide the Court with this specific power.

In my very humble opinion, the law of then and the precepts emerging were fine for the times when men (meaning humankind, to be politically correct) and mice were simple, less scheming and scandalous, and more importantly, devoid of 2020's levels of Evil.

The political weaponization against Donald Trump is sufficient grounds to revisit the following unaltered declaration, with the problem highlighted:

*If men were angels, no government would be necessary. In framing a government which is to be administered by men over men, the great difficulty lies in this: you **must first enable the government to control the governed** and, in the next place, oblige it to control itself.*

James Madison, Federalist Paper No. 51 (1788).

With due respect and humble apologies to James Madison, I have no problem with the "angels" thing because, from common wisdom, and dinned into my brains by Ricky and Elvis, is the caveat that rushing in like a fool into unchartered territory is never wise – but the old **guy** just thinks he's too **big** and won't listen (climate change for instance, by politicians and unscientific alarmists, while science is trying to establish, whether it is man, a natural cycle of heating and cooling, etc. – and by the way, no one takes the name of God here in vain, for fear of pissing Moses off.

Anyhow, here is how that should read, revamped with the Evil of today:

*If men were angels, no government would be necessary. In framing a government that is to be administered by men over men, the great difficulty lies in this: you **must first a) control the governed,** and b) in the next place, oblige it to control itself, and c). enable the government to – act in an unbiased manner, propagate the equal application of the law by the Department of Justice, hold dear the presumption of innocence, and commit to serving the country.*

Being a multi-disciplinary gent, I have borrowed from the Business Process Reengineering (BPR), that world and, pursuant to the Evil, have coined a new term, **Judicial Process Reengineering (JPR).** The radical redesign of judicial and processes of governance to achieve dramatic improvements in the eradication of evil, to aid in the unbiased and un-weaponized application of the law. Thanks. Joe, for your contribution to JPR, and legal evolution.

Simple Snoopy: Wow, LL, how wonderfully well you have reordered the priorities and the to-do list of the government, taking into consideration the current Evil! I am amazed and more Thunderstruck by you than by ACDC. But I refuse to be undone. Turning from one Big Guy to Another – Julius Caesar, and speaking about Shakespeare, Cleopatra, and Julius Caesar, how would you rearrange his famous words: "I came, I saw, I conquered?"

No hurry, take your time, and as our investigative, dapper Belgian compatriot Hercule Poirot would say: "If the little grey cells are not exercised, they grow the rust." While with each takedown, my humility takes a backseat, and I am inclined to say, Another One Bites… and another one gone Hey, I'm gonna get you, too.

We've been preaching copyright, intellectual property rights, and our fight to prevent the dishonor of plagiarism and the deceit to authors and creative artists, so I dutifully give the honors to John, Sir Brian, Freddy, and Roger for those lines and spaces, as they say in music.

Borrowing a page from JPR and Learned Lewis, I'm also going to suggest genetic testing of King Arthur Ergonomic, and his DNA, as it appears that there is a translocation of Chromosome C – the Common-Sense Chromo of the moron.

He'll need a radical restructuring as well of a combo of a bio-medical-judicial redesign that has gone mutationally haywire, perhaps just born with a congenital anomaly – see, I'm a quick learner LL, impressed? I normally do not fish for compliments; praise does egg me on, and moreover, as a team, we have to beat evil.

Chapter 5:
The Unholy and Pre-Ordained Guilty as Charged

Every citizen, from the ex-president to the common man, regardless of who the individual is, every human being is entitled to a personal defense and, more importantly, no weaponized agenda to "Get" and convict in advance, which amounts to blatant injustice and persecution. Those against, the opponents and biased expect all outside of the power sphere to submit to the bullying and intimidation.

As a human rights advocate, I (Learned Lewis) would advise any entity to defend themselves vigorously, as that is a God-given human right, set forth in the Universal Declaration of Human Rights (UDHR), proclaimed by the United Nations General Assembly in Paris on 10 December 1948.

All this nonsensical vitriol we see regarding the Trump cases is in complete mockery and denial of individual civil rights, liberties, freedoms, and rights, as enshrined in the Constitution and the Bill of Rights, insofar as equality in justice. It is currently the willful distortion of the fundamental precepts of law for manipulated electioneering and to render political opposition handicapped to the degree to be totally inconsequential. Americans' rights in relation to government and the guarantees of civil rights and liberties to the individual, notably freedom of speech, press, and due process of law and, are not just compromised and disparaged; the weaponization has sought to obliterate these fundamental rights.

Let a neutral commission investigate this post-election for purposes of research, detecting gaps and lapses, and improving the law for the people.

Not a Doomsday Book, For a Gleeful Tomorrow Instead!

This is a book for easy reading and humor, and not pure law, although appropriately infused with foundational principles of jurisprudence and law, merely to expose the frailties of human nature and convey some important concepts on which our laws are founded. This is not a Domesday Book of 2024!

This book is premised on one important fact occurring, that is the conclusion by some of the pre-ordained guilt, and of having committed crimes, therefore you have already judged. Any on-sided tainted slant is fine for a layman who is swayed by political indoctrination, but not how this should be with the learned courts, at the highest levels, and Yours Truly – Simple Snoopy and Learned Lewis.

An unbiased legal system will ideally deliver justice by examining matters without preconceived feelings one way or another. The American system of justice has evolved from the English common law, transforming into its current complex (that even befuddles legal experts) series of procedures and decisions. It does not need to argue that ethics and morality in our laws owe significantly to the underpinnings of Judeo-Christian principles, notably in 'The Rule of Law,' which is recognized as one of the pillars of American justice and democracy, until Big Evil changed the world, from 2020 to 2024, that is.

Judeo-Christian tradition is the written law code outlined in the Ten Commandments. I am not preaching religiosity here! Only drawing attention that the phrase "presumption of innocence," although not expressly written into the Constitution, is however implied, in that "due process" entails fairness, and the onus is on the government to not play dirty.

They cannot deprive you of your freedom or property with failure to follow proper procedures – not the whims of Judge Ergonomic in arbitrary and excessive punitive order for $454 million, in the absence of default, claims of fraud, or representation by financial wizards, institutions and individuals in the case of Donald Trump, in New York, which defies 'fairness' and sanity.

Due process generally means Your right to be presumed innocent until proven guilty is fundamental to due process. The presumption of innocence is a constitutional right, even if it is not directly addressed. Importantly, the presumption of innocence rests on the right and recourse to justice and to be heard, or *Audi alteram partem* (or audiatur et altera pars) - which is a Latin phrase meaning "listen to the other side," or "let the other side be heard as well" - reminds one a little of the Joni Mitchell song title "Both Sides Now."

The presumption of innocence is not guaranteed in the U.S. Constitution. However, through statutes and court decisions, several by the U.S. Supreme Court, a fair trial is expected; but frequently needs the examination of what has prompted the unfairness. The connivance, greed, political persuasions, and other forms that underlie the deviousness to frame, if uncovered carefully and diligently, will show Clever Evil!

Change: Time and Tide

We have to see greater neutrality in the legal system. As a legal mind, my analysis reveals a great deal of nasty rhetoric and sinister pre-ordained guilty, unless proven innocent syndrome, which is contrary to principled justice and plagues the system at the lower court level. Someone questioned me years ago on how I would defend the "lock her up" chants at trump rallies. My answer to that then and now remains unchanged.

Chants at any rally - regardless of candidate and party, are not the hallmarks of an unbiased democratic system. Chants of Death to America should be investigated and punished. While taking a knee is disrespect to the Flag, to the Star-Spangled Banner, and to Jimi, who played it with such respect, fire, sensitivity, and honor to the Nation!

Warping The Law and True Democracy

Many in the ranks of common people are not legally schooled, as would be in a learned judiciary that is expectedly aloof from political affiliation. At the same time, politicians must also not sound derogatory and call sections of the population names and labels such as "deplorables" based on their occupation, preferences, status, economics, or whatever else. Nevertheless, reforms are immediately necessary in the judicial system, which evolves into a mature democracy.

Unfortunately, at the time of writing this book in March-April 2024, I can see we have regressed in democratic traditions and legal values, with aberrations on both counts, and we need to unite to make this about America and the values which we are all about, notably equality unto the law, equal opportunity, and all in all, like Artificial Intelligence taking over, we have to be careful our values are never compromised, and the regress must be halted.

The presumption of guilt, from the outset (right from the beginning: Latin: *ab initio*), is a premise that it is an out-of-control and berserk perpetration, right from its earliest origins, against the very foundations of civilized law. Set it up to Convict, Somehow, get it to, even if it Don't Fit! – which worked the other way around once in the OJ Simpson case. There was a murder, gloves, a body, blood, and a crime scene. Now, here it is, different magicians, pulling out new stunts from a hat of conjured tricks and charges, with disgustingly EVIL in thought and scheme.

No Dispute

Let it be said that firstly, the election of 2020 is not disputed by Simple Snoopy and Learned Lewis. However, in those early stages when the results were coming in, the President had the right to be skeptical, because election fraud, malpractices, and irregularities are adequate reasons to see if there were errors. The unflappable and erudite Supreme Court will see the vicious political underpinnings through and through.

There is absolute immunity to be able to want to see things play out. It was a close election. The argument that he persisted in denial despite the advisors informing him of the contrary, fails to realize that there were also reports contrary as well. The then President had the immunity, authority, and right to check things out to see if there were irregularities.

Making allowance for unsureness is absolutely, and if the shoe were on the other foot, meaning of the other party, they may well have done the same. To this day, Hillary maintains the elections were stolen from her, but she gets a pass because of her political pedigree. In the weaponized process, scare tactics and everything in the book and outside of it to coerce, intimidate, and get these charges to hold are evident at these lower levels, rife with political bias and fixated on exacting crippling retribution. However, disregarding the fact that anyone is entitled to free speech or an opinion of winning when everything was still up in the air, election results-wise at that time, is an abhorrent travesty, flouting the democratic process, which has been our pride. **We can do better than this as a nation.**

Tracking the Weaponization to its Diabolical Origins!

To go after terrorists, tracking the economic or money route is one that pays dividends, which means employing the reverse engineering method to go back and see who are the brains behind the operations, and track the ring leaders and bosses. The same approach in tracking the weaponization will likely lead to the key figures behind the weaponization, which RFK Jr., Donald

Trump, and millions of Americans have said that this has never happened before and in the history of our democracy.

Our legal system is derived from English Common Law, which in turn was cohesively and formally framed into law, where the landmark the Magna Carta, in the year 1215. This was the first document to rein in the authority of the king and his government, as not above the law. The principles from the exploitation of power by the governments have been closely adhered to over the years in American Justice, in what is termed and accounted to constitute 'the rule of law,' as denoted as rights and obligations in regard to authority and people.

The Brits Still Rule: The Historic Magna Carta

Suddenly, over the last few years, the very foundations of our law appear to have experienced seismic activity and shaken to its core. The relentless going after certain individuals is shattering the confidence in our justice system. The important key elements in Article 39, Magna Carta (1215), in our personal opinion, as a direct bearing on the cases against Donald Trump, is in the embedded "in any way destroyed," as the efforts are to destroy him, in multiple ways, that would make the behaviors of Judas Iscariot and Pontius Pilates, as the most reviled, odious characters and treacherous betrayers in the history of the world, seem like petty and trifling villains.

Excerpted from the historic Magna Carta:

> "No freemen shall be taken or imprisoned or disseised or exiled **or in any way destroyed,** nor will we go upon him nor send upon him, except by the lawful judgment of his peers or by the law of the land." Article 39, Magna Carta (1215).

The weaponization seen is the most extreme snub to democracy, which needs to be traced to its core, and such evil should never in the future never allowed to rear its ugly head, regardless of who ascends the Throne, from the election in November 2024. After that, no retribution and no dictators for a day or night!

Learned Lewis and Simple Snoopy can be hired to oversee the seamless and painless transition, with Lionel Richie doing the honors with All Night Long – but we will give his vocal cords adequate rest, as we will use AI for the accompaniment of the Heavenly voicings of Guitar Gods SRV, Jimi, and Beck!

Chapter 6:
Musings II: From the Desks of Learned Lewis and Simple Snoopy

We are seeing a more a different side of Trump now in 2024. More mature, more earnest, serious, sober, and a determined solemnity to reverse the nonsense of Sleepy. From our side, we wish him nothing but the best and very well in retired life.

Hur's hauntings, and damning words, scare us that a jury would perceive the President as old and sympathetic from their conviction, is a welcome travesty. In Congress, Hur defended his report's discussion of Biden's memory by saying, "I had to show my work."

Adaptiveness, agility, and being ready to lead in the face of change are the hallmarks of the resilient, and Trump has demonstrated those qualities far better than the "sympathetic, well-meaning, elderly man with a poor memory," quoting the Hur report. Those fixated only on clinging to power fail to see change and deny the opportunities and potential for greater success of Americans than the innovative, experienced, progressive, and prosperous business-minded.

It is not the time to play games with American lives and let the unknown, unvetted, and criminals, for we do not want another Moscow, Mumbai, or Mali happening again. Haven't we learned enough from 911 already?

Innovation is not conjured from anything, and investments and a deliberate process are required to set the wheels of innovation in motion! Innovation and change are inextricably intertwined, and are needed to remedy the current state and for Trump to hit the ground running in formulating and implementing change management actions that would be necessary and also feasible. Invite the collaboration of smart people from everywhere. Create social architecture as a means to foster greater innovative and creative propensities in the country, and we'd show how as well.

Let's be preachy males (heeding the warnings of James Carville, the Democratic Strategist for the last 100 years) for a change and say that to ingrain a positive culture, one favoring continuous improvement, America needs to inculcate the value of collaboration and camaraderie. The next administration must foster social network architecture that relies on self-belief in the abundance of man and women, American talent, and their welfare and development.

Musings III: From the Desks of Learned Lewis and Simple Snoopy

To err is Human and Divine; we forgive Ole Joe, but tell him to go back now to Delaware. No time for experiments and learning from mistakes, like the fiasco in Afghanistan or the mayhem and disaster in the economy and immigration. Let's get back to striving for zero errors, or defects taught to the world by an American named Edward Deming.

Mistakes cannot be ongoing and constant, and our constant playing catch-up as a result of negligence and failure to pay attention to detail has been horrifying. Learn from winners. Take, for example, Snoop Dogg, whose net worth is in the millions.

Invite such figures and the savvy, as he has built on empire the affection of fans and followers for his talent and performance and judicious business investments. He and so many from all walks of life can assist us in smartening America to be open to all ideas in education, law, research, math, and reading.

The fear of intellectual property rights being infringed upon is a concern that often causes innovation wariness, so assure them of their value for sharing ideas for the good of the community, Americans, and the world. We need to get back to our winning ways!

Multinational companies are reluctant to secure a more extensive presence in some countries with a proven record in terms of their disregard for intellectual property rights and patent protection, turn a blind eye to blatant piracy, and exhibit a lack of reforms that would recognize and guarantee such protection.

We are sure that someone like Trump will favor the protection of investment and censure violators who cheat Americans with scams, prey on Seniors, and enrich themselves. Then there are those in the country who cleverly enhance their enormous personal wealth with fear-mongering while travelling in gas-guzzling Jets.

High Esteem, Earned with Greatly Balanced Views

Even sports columnist extraordinaire Stephen A. Smith is upset and declared he's 'ashamed' of the Democratic Party for not replacing Biden, calling it 'pathetic.' But wait a minute, one with a sharp tongue, you are stereotyping if you say as a Black man, it is not OK to vote for Trump. C'mon man. Shed these old-fangled, narrow-minded notions. Nobody is beholden to the Democratic Party. We are one America, and people's lives matter. As a leader, you cannot discredit good men like Ben Carson, Tim Scott, Larry Elder, Leo Terrell, Marco Rubio, Ramaswamy, and even hesitant Haley and Tuppence will come around, and others from the other side of the aisle as well.

Overly praise nor any negative views of Stephen Smith are intended and premature by anyone! He has matured, and we consider him a revered sportscaster but also a balanced leader with mature, unbiased views that clearly show an America First attitude and recognition of the potential of all.

Quit the Dislike and Unite for America

Mike Pense, Nikki Haley, Chris Christie, and also the fair-minded from the Democratic Party set aside love and hate, come together for humanity now! Who will want to prevent the unmitigated disaster from continuing? But you are right, Stephen Smith, a voice of reason. 'You can't stop him. You cannot stop him,' as you said about Trump, because it is America. But is it still the land of the free and the home of the brave?

The answer is not blowing in the wind – it is an emphatic No! We need to come together as a nation and rededicate ourselves on the path of righteousness. It's Now or Never!

Nobody is perfect, but no human being should have their human rights violated to the extent it is happening – All and minorities, it is time to rally together for justice and rights against the excessive force of the powerful exerted against those whom they want to suppress. What separates us for now from being a Banana Republic is that this opponent has not been subjected to torture and physical abuse, but the legal and psychological warfare is arguably as horrendous, and some may say more damaging and horrifying.

With a level of unprecedented persecution, as American, regardless of race, color, creed, and all other affiliations and associations, we should be ashamed of ourselves. We call Donald Trump, the **Bravest Man in the World**, to have survived this onslaught and vilification.

The Case Against Donald Trump is a Human Rights Issue

The tirelessly excellent work of the former longest-serving First Lady, Eleanor Roosevelt, in the framing and development of the Universal Declaration of Human Rights (UDHR) is suddenly cast asunder. Although established in response to the atrocities during WWII and the Holocaust, it must be amended in light of the persecution here.

Most people will not know that in the definition and types of human rights violations, the actions and misdeeds of the state are included. A state and its agencies commit human rights violations either directly or indirectly, unintentionally or intentionally, and the latter seems to be true for the last four years.

The deliberate engagement of the state in actions that degrade the human life of an individual is a serious violation. The violation is even more serious when the entire government machinery of judges, prosecutors, government officials, and others are orchestrated to act with singular intent – against one man. Although some charges may have merit when compounded in the manner as has been, they lack convincing the world other than political spite in fear for several reasons that are cited in this book.

Normally, it is the duty of the state to protect individuals and groups. Here, there is an aberration to that bounden duty. Here, the state itself is the perpetrator, unfortunately. The evil plots emanating from the uppermost echelons here have crossed the thresholds and distinctions of civil, political, economic, cultural, and social rights insofar as the human rights violations of the aggrieved.

The rights enshrined in the Universal Declaration of Human Rights and in the legally binding International Covenants of Human Rights (ICCPR, CESCR) are transgressed here in respect of equality before the law, the right to a fair trial, and psychological torture and economic punitive intentions that equate to physical torture and arbitrary arrest. The latter is blatant election interference by willful design intended to prevent campaigning by the party in power and an explicit suppression of political rights.

The higher ideals of the UNDHR and the treaty itself have been ratified by the United States, which was made possible by leaders such as Eleanor Roosevelt. We are failing in something we ourselves professed and committed to treasure, honor, and safeguard. The right of the people of the United States is to hold the government responsible for this slippage from Human Rights pioneers to that of a violator of the rights of an individual. Normally, it is the responsibility of the government to intervene and prosecute those responsibly; here, it is deplorable that it is itself guilty of infringement.

With a Little Help, Come Together as a Nation!

While we have sung the praises of the late Eleanor Roosevelt, not to make light of the terrible injustice, we cannot help ourselves by making reference to the late Eleanor Rigby, as well as to the wonderful strings and orchestration, the wonderful voices and harmony. It can also provide us with inspiration, for if we 'Come Together' right now as a Nation, we will not be all the lonely people, no matter where we come from or belong. Sir Paul and John are great visionaries. I'm sure that a little help from these friends is appreciated. Ironically, little would they envision that Liverpudlian words may be a rallying call for American Greatness and Unity as we see it.

Chapter 7:
What Matters Most to Americans: Cost of Food on the Table!

What matters most to Americans are the "Bear Necessities." Not enormous amounts of honey and gargantuan quantities of food for hibernation, but just enough to get by for the week and not live paycheck-to-paycheck – which is currently difficult for many. If it weren't for Food Stamps' generous donations, the situation would be as dire as "Give us this Day, Our Daily Bread."

Forget all the fancy and misplaced talk from the two corners of the mouths of politicians in power and their brainwashed loudmouths. It costs more to put food on the table now than ever before. Do a comparison for yourself, and don't be n denial!

The caption on an article read: "As Trump romps to wins, anti-Trump Republicans wonder: Do I still have a political home?" Needless to say, such a form of both sides now, investigative and research-oriented journalism is meant to provoke nasty discourse, as did with this encounter, we report here:

Unafraid Reports of Truthfulness

Armstrung, a gentleman, clearly out of touch with earthly reality, had just returned from celestial orbit. He started blaming quite creatively the "orange messiah" and "Mango Mussolini" - the former President for the rise in prices to the Saudis with the closure of refineries, deliberate oversupply of oil in the midst of pandemic-related shutdowns, and OPEC+ production cuts, and "turmoil" in the Red Sea.

Fact Check, Armstrung was told: Gas prices were way lower then, as we were even exporting. Inventory and grocery prices are related to gas prices. Ole reversed the policy on gas. With him now on the losing streak and slipping in the polls to the lowest ever, he has changed course on oil and energy in the last few months.

On the first day, one created light and the other darkness. And God said, "Let there be light," and there was light. God saw that the light was good, and he separated the light from the darkness. God called the light "day," and the darkness he called "night." In contrast, pandering to the extreme left and the green zealots, over-smart President Biden's first day in office, created darkness, as he shut down the Keystone XL pipeline and eliminated 11,000 good-paying American jobs, with the stroke of a pen.

Simple Snoopy: Klondike Kate, you couldn't be the UK wrestler, who is plenty smart. Just as I thought, you have no knowledge of economics and energy. Oil production is not attributed to Ole McDuck, who cut down production and shut pipelines. He reversed his stance once he saw it jeopardizing his re-election chances.

The politics of oil are particularly tricky for Ole and the Party as the aim in the 2024 elections is to woo young, climate-conscious voters to come out in big numbers. Most who want to hear efforts are to keep oil in the ground. It is not going to work, as young workers are seeing that a) gas, food, and inflation under Biden are scary for them, b) Electric Vehicles are not living up to their touted promise, and c) Trump is youthful in outlook and is determined to advance America's fortunes, while Biden is past his prime and time, and the future under him appears dismal.

Strange Brew: Comparisons of Guitar God and Prince of Evil

The prices can be even further lowered, and Americans can be kept safer - however, ole senile began his presidency as the man who thought he knew too much, pressured really by other voices, but he'd never admit it because he's in a daze, a purple haze, all in his brain. Guitar God Jimi's words say it all about Joe's current decline, dementia, and evil devilishness to go after his opponents.

Purple haze all in my brain;

Lately, things just don't seem the same

Actin' funny, but I don't know why;

'Scuse me while I kiss the sky

Purple haze all around; Don't know if I'm comin' up or down

(You've gone up, Joe, and what goes up must come down, so said Isaac Newton and Blood, Sweat & Tears, and they can't be wrong. Am I happy or in misery? (You are happy, but America is in misery).

Whatever it is, that girl put a spell on me. Not one girl, but the Squad.

So, **Klondike Kate:** Here is never presented before trivia of God Jimi, and Sinner Joe:

Jimi and Joe were just born a week apart:

Jimi: November 27, 1942 | Joe: November 20, 1942.

Jimi, poet, Guitar God | Joe, Prophet of Gloomy Doom, unless he is voted out in 2024!

Policy Ignorance Just to Be Polar Bear Opposite

Canceling the Keystone XL pipeline was only the first of many attacks from this administration on American energy production. Since then, President Biden's anti-American energy actions have included pure ignorance of science.

This sent a signal—the wrong signal—that the Biden administration would make it harder for American energy producers, refiners, and workers to unleash domestic production.

Originally, he was to 'phase' it out. In 2019, the then-former vice president and Democratic presidential candidate at a New Hampshire called the young woman "kiddo" and said, "I want you to look at my eyes. I guarantee you. I guarantee you. We're going to end fossil fuel."

A year previous, Letticia James made an election promise of a different kind – to "Get Trump and Family." I'm not trying to influence voting here, but with senility apparent, Smiley is ready and praying for a default Pres sooner rather than later.

Life and Let Live: Let All Technologies Evolve Man!

Common sense is needed to Live and Let Live. What that means is to let science and technological innovation advance simultaneously in the agenda and the drive towards lowering costs and compliance with stringent emission controls. This can be simultaneously and in parallel with electric vehicle development, rather than the prognosticators of gloom and doom and shut-downs fueled by a combo of ignorance and stupidity, goring us to death with fear, causing upheaval and scare for devious political intentions, to hang on sloppily to power.

Politicians cannot set targets and timelines on climate change when there isn't conclusive prove to indicate whether it is due to greenhouse emissions, a natural phase the earth is going through, or any other explanations. Therefore, to arbitrarily shut down industries with no proven rationale is questionable, as unqualified quacks become overnight champions and experts with great visions of sacks of money – remember the Beagle Boys?

Cutting U.S. greenhouse emissions in half by 2030, with elimination by 2050, is laudable, but not one versus the other. Fear Gore-mongering on the unknown, and with other major economies doing their own thing, is indication enough that not all are on the same page on what is touted as strategies to avert the most deadly and costly effects of climate change. The solution – Live and Let Live – with continuous improvement and ongoing research and learning for all existing and emerging technologies, and not the ideas of Old Fartsy!

Optimizing oil efficiencies in engines, alternate sources of energy, and electric vehicles can all evolve at the time and point when the advances with naturally cause the inefficient to "phase out" rather than politically driven, un-engineered, and non-scientific backgrounds to use this for personal gain.

Making money in oil and energy overseas, but in the United States, trying to shut it down is duplicitous and with likely disingenuous intentions. Shut it down here, so there are deals overseas, eh? Let all technologies exist and evolve to the point of their own demise and market-driven life cycles.

America Last, Innovation Pioneering Disruptor

As Americans, we know that "Change" is ongoing and allows only the complacent to rest on their laurels. Time does not diminish the value of an invention and an innovation and usually spurs the development of further improvements in offshoots, generations, versions, and possibly new offerings in products and services. Inventions and innovations inspire the creative spirit and human intellect.

Some of the greatest innovations and innovations are known to mankind have been "Born in the USA," from Hollywood and entertainment to biomedical discovery and electronic engineering. The ingenuity and toil of Americans, our progression and evolution manifest in achievement, all possibly with the right amount of praise, rewards, incentives, and the quest for the best, which calls for business ideas, not old political ideas and hate speech.

Futuristic visionaries like Steve Jobs and Gates and other pioneers did not call for the shut-down of other industries: "People don't know what they want until you show it to them. That's why I never rely on market research. Our task is to read things that are not yet on the page." (Steve Jobs). Presidents, current and former, are not geniuses like Steve Jobs; they must create jobs and not take these away! Innovation and change go hand in hand, but politicians cannot suddenly show up and decide to close and shut down industries. **It is for innovation to be disruptive, not politicians.**

Start of An Earthly Discourse: Crime and Mayhem

Here comes along this gent **Kris-Kross** (called him Kristofferson) telling me to stop "moaning and whining" about the illegal immigrants flooding the country and questioning even my vocabulary because I often use disguised words to beat the AI filters online. He even told me that I possibly needed help to make it through nights and days. Since I only longed for the good days of old, which had all that soul.

Hey man, I am in favor of using the powers of critical thinking and immense discernment, steeped in literature (Elizabethan to contemporary) and science. Quoting Wadsworth doesn't impress Canadian Shania or me. Humanity for immigrants is and was already there. We are known to be a generous nation. Policies are making us lawless with defunding the Police. Overall, rotten to the core policies with that warped sense of socialism cause a loss of family values and broken families, which lead to more single moms and fatherless teens.

Why should there be humanity for "illegals" with criminal histories and undocumented and unknown origins fake asylum seekers from over 100 countries, many hostile to us? Send them back, just as India, Pakistan, Canada, Australia, and others do. There is a process - abide by the law, apply, qualify, and do not come here to rip off the American taxpayer - it is not about moaning and whining, but rather upsetting our way of life and building a bank of future voters – who are you kidding 'For the Good Times man? There ain't none now.

Depression with Poll Number, Resort to Ugly Name Calling:

The quick "MAGA-MAGA" name-calling is pure nonsense for anyone with a different viewpoint, meant to silence and intimidate, but rest assured, comparisons of Trump to Hitler may work for the weak, the gullible, not a powerful voice such as this, who dispassionately views facts, data, info/details, the law, demographic trends, economic key performance factors, etc. So, composer (I took it that the gent was stealing the identity of the "Help Makie it Through the Night" composer dude), do mull over carefully all said. An educated response is possibly outside capability for your party blinders, preventing the lens of truth and reality from shining through.

Donald Trump was expressing to all New York courts of unwillingness and inability to post the $464 million appeal bond to offset the massive civil fraud penalty leveled against him by the state in February of 2024. The new revelation, on social media of having the cash, which was at hand and intended use in his presidential campaign, met with all kinds of nasty diatribes before and after, for which DT should be complimented for keeping everyone and the hate-filled second-guessing in style – a suspense and a horror movie, all in one.

MAD Maddison, his name on social media, said, "Trump should have known better. This moment was going to happen for years now. He should have prepared for this fine, and why should he complain that it's all last minute? On March 24, 2024, my response was, "How do you know what he knew or knows, moron? Are you a mind reader or something to know what he thinks? He's got fleets of limos to ferry legal eagles wherever Joe's bunch have tried to set illegal traps.

Gospel John came along to snidely preach his sermon on 20 March 2024 and said, "We know Trump it's pretty awesome, has messed with financial laws for decades, thinking he'd never get caught, but finally did catch up with him." HUZZAH.

Snoopy Reply and Response: Wow, I said, "You are deviating from spreading the word of God and spewing sewage from Galilee to NY now. There were no complaints or default delinquency reported by financial institutions and aggrieved parties, including the IRS. The holy man of the New Testament angrily retorted, "Maybe you should make a mad dash to NY and give Trump's inept lawyers a hand in straightening all this out then."

Jospel, I advise in the USA and worldwide! No need to make sane and mad Door Dashes Helter Skelter! Thus, for instance, I will advise Ole to step down from the throne for a younger person, as his policies are ruining America. In the age of AI, we do not want someone who thinks in terms of record players, faxes, and gramophones.

Gospel John, 'quite an irrelevant remark and pretty funny. Good grief, record players, and vinyl are making such a huge comeback. Maybe that old-school way of doing things isn't as outdated or undesirable as you think. I will agree with you 100% that we need age restrictions. And term limits to the office."

Illegal Immigration and Open Defecation

Simple Snoopy: I replied, what a relevant comment; the vinyl comeback is a stylus without needles; the epidemic of Fentanyl and needles is ruining the country. Look at the defecation and people on the streets – Tent Cities and the next epidemic waiting to happen.

We do not need age restrictions for running for the office. We, however, do have leaders who can walk straight, talk without a flutter and a stammer, have policies to keep the country safe, and are not using the system for political mileage and advantage – aka hanging on for dear life to the throne.

Gospel John, putting his spin: Dude, please. I'm really not sure what it is that you're actually trying to say. There has been defecation and people on the streets since the very beginning of this country without any pauses ever. Maybe sober up and try again later.

Simple Snoopy: My reply: Let the lack of education you portray have a sobering effect on you, such that it hastens your need to take free online (MOOC) courses and curb the massive ignorance on display.

Gospel, your grade is a D- Minus. No need to provide me with a list of the 10 great things happening in the country. Apparently, a lack of education buries the truth, and being in denial of the decline of America serves no purpose either. Disoriented, the name is Laken Hope Riley, and it is not Lincoln - who is no longer speaking about crime. Enroll in law and other classes – you need the education and uncommonly-common sense.

Did you see that in Florida, the State's largest police union made a major endorsement in the 2024 presidential race? Why? Because the country is in decline, hastened by poor governance and policies. The law-and-order situation is deteriorating – marauding gangs are seen looting stores, and cops are leaving and reigning *en* masse. Don't be in denial - think country first, then party, and last, Ole and Smiley!

Gospel John to Snoopy: Have you come from Mars? You speak like a Martian.

Simple Snoopy: Gospel, don't try that BS with me. I'll teach ya English all the way from the language, literature, and lingo of the Elizabethan era, from Johnson, Milton, and Shakespeare, to what we speak in the Bronx, Baptizer man. When showing the paucity of education or failure to look at the other side, you resort to insults and excuses, aka 'clutching at straws' to feign knowing.

Leave the Sea of Galilee and the fish farm for knowledge outside of the vet. Science and Baptism, and see the world, but don't abandon Jesus' man and be a disloyal politician! I'm showing you up terribly for the world to see! Get the education - will offer a tuition-free scholarship if the high school grades are decent!

Replying to Snoopy: Showing me up? You haven't even managed to show up - you couldn't teach a fish to swim.

Replying to Gospel John: No, I wouldn't teach a fish to swim; leave that to you. Do you teach fish to swim? Wow, what a preacher, man mermaid.

Chapter 8:
Who We as Americans Are! (And Who We Are Not!)

We will get Learned Lewis to explain Who We as Americans Are! (And Who We Are Not!)

Learned Lewis: The contrived political evil maneuvers of the justice system against Donald Trump are, with each passing day, quite clear that behind the weaponization lies the Hand of a Higher Evil Power with a High IQ at the lowest levels! He needs to be dethroned and is certainly not the Hand of God, who is just, forgiving, and is for all. It is called a God of set up to "Get," using every possible means, unfortunately, which we call in our everyday and simple terms: By Hook or By Crook.

The term "innocent until proven guilty" is not explicitly stated and found in the U.S. Constitution. It is the most important principle, enshrined and embedded in our system of justice nevertheless, which should never be misused and abused, but it is, through scheming and contrived "Dirty Tricks, and not Done Dirt Cheap," because the DOJ has the money and resources to pull off legal stunts, which are not only a miscarriage of justice but taints the very foundations and core of who we are as a democracy; and fine traditions as a nation. A new and absolute low and vile, sinking to the depths of corruption, intimidation, and abuse or all, and is a contradiction to any semblance and notions of fair play.

Wait a minute, it is not fair play we are talking about, but rather foul play. C'mon man, as Joe would say, the great haste to bring a multitude of more fictitious charges against Donald Trump is as plain as daylight, intention to paralyze him with lawsuits, fines, censures, and every legal impediment and obstacle possible. No doubt, with the premise, we will handcuff him figuratively. Election interference is, at its worst, a political foe.

The American people are not that gullible and are now "Beginning to See the Light." Even the haters of Donald Trump should grudgingly, and in their hearts of hearts, secretly admire his guts – for its steady resolve in Triumph for Trump, but the road of potholes, assholes (Snoopy told me to put this in), and dirt, gets smoother each day.

The usual haters say, oh well, if he is innocent, there is nothing to fear. Why is he delaying things? For those ridiculous arguments, here are just two answers to keep it short and sweet:

1. When the foundations on which these cases are built and presented are inherently flawed, the onus or responsibility rests on higher-level courts of appeal to make careful judicial determinations and pronouncements. It is not a rush to judgement, as these are not the everyday thing. These cases are not simple criminal and civil ones, for here, the interpretations must be through the lenses of jurisprudence, Constitutional Law, Civil, Criminal, and a variety of legal perspectives and take into consideration the spectrum of legal precedent and unchartered legal territory. The entire chapter is one sordid affair with the "odor of mendacity." Thanks to Judge McAfee for making this phrase, now of everyday

parlance, to show extreme deceitfulness, and would add to that disgust as well of not just Fani but the entire spectacle of hypocrisy, lies, and untruthfulness.

2. People for both sides of the aisle and the undecided and party-less or third-party proponents, by now, should know that the life of Donald Trump is about "Winning" big. He's shown that he'll do everything it takes to be successful in his legal cases, which have no merit to them, in any case. Winning is in his DNA and in his personality – **Donald Trump wants America to Prosper and Thrive. Painful and painstaking as it has been for him, he is solidly for America.**

Violation of the Presumption of Innocence

The inalienable right of every person accused of a crime is to be presumed innocent till his or her guilt is established beyond a reasonable doubt. The concern here in the cases against former President Trump is for the extraordinary lengths these weaponized and contrived charges have been framed and that these are for political gain and mileage at a level and degree unprecedented and never seen before.

Shame on the DOJ. For they thought that by throwing enough shit at the wall, most of it would stick, and Trump would be embroiled in mountainous litigation and fines, that the election would be well-nigh impossible – their aim. Cut this out, Garlic; the American people can see through you and the evil machinations.

This is far more deadly than the "axis of evil" ever was – used by President George W. Bush and originally referred to Iran, Iraq, and North Korea. How so? Here you are in violation of human decency, barbarously and unabashedly going after an American President because you fear that the dismal performance of your administration is going to be a loss in the November 2024 Presidential Elections. The weaponization is from the 'Axle of Evil,' the rotations of which are conspiratorial in trying to Get and Constrict President Donald Trump!

But the plotter and planners (whomever they may be, and surely there are some big names involved, lending their ideas and contributions to set this in motion) miscalculated on a grand scale. The old James Hadley Chase novel: 'The Way the Cookie Crumbles' is a good book of twists and turns, and the lesson is that **Evil Never Succeeds.** Hence it is in the title of this book: **Donald Trump the Bravest Man in the World - Overcoming All Odds & Evil for America.**

The DOJ agenda is clear: to throw and throw unimaginable charges across multiple fronts relentlessly and see what sticks. The notion is:

He who has Flung enough Dung will have their Victim Stung and Hung!

Keep Throwing, some will Stick, some will Fall,

Never Stop, for, in the end, you've covered the Wall

Your intended target will Cower in Fear and feel Insecurely Small

Heave your Chest with Pride, then Move in to Kill Him, their family, and 'em All

Debilitate, Damage, Take Him Down – Somehow, and Anyway! Get Him!

Damage, paralyze, care less if everything comes to a grinding halt, 'Big' Boss says, Do Whatever it Takes; the throne of Midas cannot be in jeopardy. Trump, in an April rally, said that Joe is Midas, except everything "he touches he turns to shit."

The American people now see President Trump as the Martyr and Victim. Each conviction or indictment is a badge of honor, and is met with the surge in Poll Numbers. African Americans, Hispanic/Latinos, musicians, singers, athletes, rap artists, and everyone else will always support the underdog whom the administration is trying to suppress.

America doesn't like this, Joe. Big Mistake! Regret and Apologize! It will show you to be the Big Guy. Forget the other pseudonyms! America Forgives Easily, but doesn't Forget! We'll do both for you! We'll not hold your age against you!

These contrived and frankly many of which are frivolous charges, somehow and creatively made to fit, are with the sole intention of preventing him from contesting the elections for the President of the United States in November 2024. You are a scared Bunny who cannot hop.

In a legal context, the presumption of innocence alone may be adequate grounds to cast reasonable doubt and require the acquittal of a defendant. The defendant, therefore, has the benefit of that presumption, and the burden must be on the prosecution to lay and frame the charges, to persuade that these are built on a solid foundation and can show the guilt of that charge beyond a reasonable doubt. None of this has happened in any of the cases. The charges are flimsy fallacious, and do not rise to the level of a felony.

America Can See It – Biased Juries in New York or Anywhere, make a case for judicial reform. The right to a fair trial is impossible, although there should not be one in the first place.

Doesn't Mean a Thing if it Ain't Got that Swing. Sir Duke and Ella will come to Beat Someone, and make Take the A Train or come in a Caravan to do this.

As Learned Lewis, let me unassumingly say that I am sufficiently knowledgeable about the law and hereby declare that you should know that the presumption of innocence is recognized as a due process right under the Fifth Amendment. The prosecutor has the burden of proof to meet that standard. That there is explicit guilt of the accused (criminal) or defendant (civil) case or suit, beyond a reasonable doubt – if not, you have magically arrived at something that is ethically and morally dishonorable. Alvin and the Chipmunks must read to show and have failed, so now skating on thin ice! Why not get acquainted with the DISTRICT ATTORNEYS ASSOCIATION OF THE STATE OF NEW YORK: "The Right Thing." Ethical Guidelines for Prosecutors.

Hate Mongers, Go Bonkers!

Stingray: I'll take great delight and hope with much gloating that "Rich-guy Donald Trump can't find the money for bond. How about a MAGA bake sale."

Simple Snoopy: Such barbed comments are always pathetic, as the brainwashed have not attempted to shed their wholesome lacunae in knowledge.

Learned Lewis: In days leading up to the deadline for the bond to appeal (Tue 19 Mar 2024 05:24:36 PM), and successfully lowered. The one-sided mob prompted comparisons to the Guillotine crowd, and storming the Bastille is apt. Those were the days of no trials, summary executions, no defense, convict in advance, and a gory death at the Guillotine. What inhumane savagery then and now!

For readers, the French Revolution, which lasted from 1789- 1794, was known as the "Reign of Terror." It's pretty much similar to the 'Reign of Terror.' Joe, for all his political opponents, pretends, but all 10 fingers point straight back. **Ironically, (may sound funny) political opponents in the United States are now seeking asylum in America itself,** turning to the higher courts of appeal as the lower ones are manipulated and machinated.

The Guillotine was an instrument used to carry out summary executions and capital punishment and was used to execute thousands of people, including King Louis XVI and Marie-Antoinette. In civil and military jurisprudence, summary execution refers to putting to death a person accused of a crime without the benefit of a free and fair trial.

In this book, refers to the hasty and nasty rush to judgment, to convict in the court of public opinion, as well as the weaponized judicial system by the lower courts and legal system, that shows. Education needs to be imparted, and the civilization of justice, democracy, and the rule of law taught to the hordes – 'Here, There, and Everywhere' as the Beatles would say! To this, even an ardent confirmed supporter (Yes, man) of the Democratic party and a skeptic conceded, "You won't get an argument from me! You are good!"

The before and after are remarkable, as the revelry at impending doom creates a firestorm of vile speech, which soon turns glum, smirking, with change, as one can when indoctrinated, and the reverse occurs, rather than a foregone conclusion and expected doom. Anything contrived and fabricated is going to be taken down eventually, as happens when built on the foundations of fallaciousness and falsity by and at the right levels of truth and fair play.

"The Right Thing" Ethical Guidelines for Prosecutors

The news was out in bold that Donald Trump had until Monday, March 25, 2024, to pay the $454 million bond to appeal and owed to New York, a perfect opportunity for those who take joy in the woes and plight of others. The revenge was on the cards. Attorney General Letitia James was ready to file judgments in Westchester County, where Trump has a golf resort and private estate.

What is remarkable is that it is easy for some to disavow oaths to uphold the law, as many never miss an opportunity to (shamelessly) steal some airplay. Later, the bond amount on successful appeal to the ridiculous, shameful amount by Ergonomic and Wilting Lettuce was reduced by 60%.

Simple Snoopy and I would not have let this get this far! All gets thrown out now or on appeal, hopefully. Simple Snoopy says the Prosecutor must feel the heat, I would think, that they could scarcely sleep a Wink, for each night could wake up in a Cold Seat for Uneasy lies the head that wears a Guilded Crown and matching Trousers and Trident.

Also, please read the entire guidelines, "Ethical violations expose prosecutors to formal discipline including censure, suspension, and disbarment; case-specific sanctions, such as reversal of convictions, preclusion of evidence, and dismissal of charges; and employment sanctions, including damaged reputation, loss of effectiveness, demotion, and termination." DISTRICT ATTORNEYS ASSOCIATION OF THE STATE OF NEW YORK, **"The Right Thing," Ethical Guidelines for Prosecutors**.

Michael Tells Luco to Make this Hateful an Offer.

The Luco, referred to is the one who had pledged his "ever-ending loyalty," but erred down the line. Now, here comes former principal deputy solicitor general and lawyer Neal Katyal telling a known compatriot vilified Psaki on a weekly meet that he's 'Don Poorleone' Because 'He Can't Get the Money' for New York Fraud Penalty. Aside from desperately trying always to stay relevant, perhaps this immigrant wants to show he's every bit American – but that is not how America is.

Someone remarked you follow the money trail to get crooks and terrorists, but with that curved, crooked, cutthroat Cutyal, you follow the camera, and he'll be there, yes, he will, because he ain't no friend of real justice! Irreverential and clueless, he's no doubt also oblivious really about the Godfather, Brandon, who spoke softly, with love, as the man and the character, as did Andy, who sang softly, and Al Martino, for him at the wedding.

Millionaire Jimmy, with Some Big Shipments

So, the long and repetitive DT hate content, was usually met with not so dignified contempt of Wow for Millionaire Jimmy by Simple Snoopy! So many lines to express so little! Take a course on succinct writing, man! Betta still just keeps selling pizzas for tips, Jimmie, man!

But acerbic Jimmie claimed to be a retired millionaire who likes giving pizza away and even goes to deliver it from time to time to make people smile and show some love! His words, MAGA, are always pointing fingers, hiding, and deflecting with the criminal treasonous trump, a bad choice! Vote Blue Keep America Great. Stop Grifters and Traitors! Trump For Prison Showers 2024.

Simple Snoopy in a scathing rebuke: What was the big deal made on Coke, fakey millionaire? Millionaires don't brag, even if you have a few remarkable shipments. Be careful, man; a trail is always left behind, and One Way or Another, they're gonna get you! Ask Blondie!

As an independent favoring the rule of law, I will support incarceration if they catch you! Vote for good policy and not color, Red or Blue. Good policy is keeping us safe and free, with no wars and goodies to terrorists, as we did in Afghanistan and Iran, and for heaven's sake, affordable food on the table.

Peggy Sue: Then, before March 24, Peggy Sue (Yeah, think she got married) starts the DT revulsion conversation stream: "Ms. James, get the plane as one of your first seizures! He'll not travel privately. It'll be fun to watch a commercial while standing in line. Ha! Won't it!

Then, a few vicious males (**Marcus Aurelius**, notably) say that they will even urinate on his grave and on his star in Hollywood, which is truly unforgivable. I'm sure that the other side never says such extreme and horrible things about Joe.

Aurelius was reminded that he was not immortal, using his own words of not "going to live ten thousand years. Death hangs over you," and, "While you live, while it is in your power, be good."

Simple Snoopy: Peggy Sue, wow, you take great glee at the plight of others, eh? You've heard that wish others harm, and it comes back to haunt ya - or what goes around, turns around and hits you in the face!

I reminded the bunch of Newton's Third Law: Action and Reaction: That for every action (force) in nature, there is an equal and opposite reaction, which means that **you urinators, that could mean people taking a dump on your graves! That may have scared them shitless,** for there was no talk of that after that.

After the bond was reduced by 60%, I asked Peggy Sue to follow the boys and stand in line to pee, with no exceptions, and sitting was'nt allowed. With 60% saved on the bond, they will invest a small amount to come to do this on you. Raincoats and umbrellas will offer no protection.

Lady Renegade, however, did not take kindly to the admonition: "You seem to have difficulty accepting a fact of criminality. They must do that in your country of Russia. You seem so familiar with the process."

Simple Snoopy: You need a geography lesson, Renegade Lady. In Russia, there's no rain, just Ice, Snow, and Putin. The plains of Spain, where the rain is mainly confined, are far away, and so are the monsoons of India. Nothing good comes from evil. Santana and Pete Green have been saying this from the sixties and Woodstock. Preaching criminality is only the None on the View.

The None is an oddity, really. We don't reveal our race, but we can say with confidence that the world loves African Americans. From Dizzy, Miles, Armstrong, Joplin, Charlie Christian, Coleman Hawkins, Tatum, Garner, BB, Bessie, Nat, and Jimi, to Money, Tyson, Robinson, Leonard, Mosley, Witherspoon, Mercer, Holyfield, Bowe, Toney, Jones, Hopkins, Shavers, Norton, Smokin Joe, Forman, Ali, Jordan, James, and an endless list of entertainers, sportsmen, and the best of best as humans too. Therefore, for someone who has done much for all Americans of all races and nationalities, to make stupid comments like 'We Can Put You in Jail for Your Entitlements' is horrid and unfortunate.

Don't Let the Odd Rotten Apple in a Barrel Retard Good Change

The intense hate is remarkable by the odd rotten apple in any barrel of society. We need a new tomorrow to thrive and not survive as costs escalate and rise, curbing the fueling of heat and animosity. A businessman rather than a career politician will douse the flames of inequality, be the spark to ignite positive change for all and forge a path to the betterment of all.

Americans are the finest people in the world. It is politicians who derail our aspirations and short-circuit our opportunities and talents with policies that aim to protect their interests, legacies, and fuel economic avariciousness. Money makes the politician go; forget mares!

Nuns, None, and Bad Habits

The original and real always. The Real Catholic nun, Mother Miriam, has seen through the shenanigans of "evil" Biden and, in March 2024, has supported the reelection of the former for legal and not expedited, voter fraud list creation to win elections with non-citizens. All evil tricks to cover up.

Simple Snoopy: Goldberg None, with the Bad Habit of advancing racial animosity, is a well-known, who needs education and reverse DEI training. Anyone not African American is sure to invite her wrath with a pompous show and air akin to Oh, tell me all about it. I am the final word and deed, with or without the Habit.

It's small wonder the smart ex-governor and Ambassador, then Presidential candidate Haley, reacted to this one of the several extreme left, patronizing spews of The View' hosts against the other side, vilifying African Americans and all others for their mere association with Trump. Haley was right in saying: 'I did a whole lot more than Whoopi Goldberg will ever do.'

The Zenith of Political Hate!

The extreme manifestation of political hate. Hang your heads in shame, for on Tuesday, Mar 26, 2024, NBC News sacked, almost immediately, hiring the former Republican National Committee chair, Ronna McDaniel, as a paid political analyst. This morally wicked and reprehensible act has given a human being a black eye, with the backlash from the network's leading sanctimonious and preachy anchors. Rona should easily prevail in a lawsuit.

The 2020 election was not subverted. It has the winner in office for almost 4 years, who has failed miserably and dismally. Since when are anchors recruitment and human resource managers? Their same sanctimonious and preachy style of Morning, Noon, and Night and Mad Doe is all that signifies malicious efforts in imposition of their views. Truly regrettable in a democracy.

An Exception to Every Rule

At least, an exception, when 'The 'View' co-host Alyssa Farah Griffin, a Trump aide got it right. Here, appreciation of Donald Trump's attending the funeral of a slain officer in New York endeared him more to voters than President Biden's celebrity-filled campaign fundraiser was accurate. But she'd better be careful because there's zero tolerance for any Americans outside the party, just like they undid the shoelaces of Lady Rona McDaniel at the other place.

Americans of every race and nationality will shun the cheap shot racial animus directly by Fani Willis, Letticia, and Bragg because the future can be assuredly brighter when there is independence of the judiciary from politics (Ergonomic, are you listening before your unscheduled visit to the psych)?

Set political persuasions and affiliations aside, recuse rather than partake in weaponization and tainted directives from wherever they may come, and learn from the nobility in judicial uprightness exemplified by learned justices overseas. A shining example is Chief Justice Chandrachud of India, who is intelligent, unbiased, and a legal scholar to the hilt.

America is Holding You to Higher Ethical, Moral, and Legal Standards

Lest you forget, your accountability to America! Rein in the pride, and don't overstep your boundaries. The laughing stock of the world for 450 million + bond, unheard of, and a disgrace to justice in the USA and the conduciveness of business in America and New York – You give Justice a Bad Name. We have to be content now simultaneously with sanity and senility, and Americans, of the informed and prudent kind, will discern truth from keeping a candidate away from elections and say **Enough is Enough,** morons.

Never Again in America!

The imperatives are stark! Examine afresh directives, edicts, guidelines, laws, and codes of conduct in light of these officials in 2023-2024 in improvement. Judicial officials need training and new guidelines to ensure judicial independence and integrity. Screen for political bias, as well as using the judicial process and lessons from victims and scapegoats at the receiving end of prosecutorial and judicial misconduct in subtle and open malafide exemplification, as lessons in evil practice avoidance.

Never again must such grand-scale weaponization occur in this country!

Whether it is a Board of Commissioners on Grievances and Discipline in an independent board appointed by the Supreme Courts of States to guide and instill ethical and professional standards for judges and attorneys, there are clearly 'Gaps' between the current and desired state. The Code of Conduct for United States Judges and the underlying ethical canons that guide judges perhaps can be infused with multidisciplinary knowledge, and here is a suggestion.

Recommendation for Academic Research

A recommendation (one way – consult LL and Snoopy) to achieve this impartiality may be to adopt and train judges in a technique used by qualitative researchers called bracketing. It is the setting aside of one's personal own beliefs, preconceived notions, and prior assumptions by writing these down, placing them within brackets, and making a determined effort to ensure that these will not interfere in decision-making and in the interpretation of data and experiences. An absolutely wonderful tool for these codes of conduct to be infused and training of existing and future judges in order to avoid misrepresenting a subject's intended meaning, perception, or experience.

With bracketing, Bragg, Vengeance Merchant, Ergonomic, Lettuce, and Venus may have to undergo training on the sanctity of judicial fairness and independence to ensure no further miscarriage of justice and set aside their political leanings and tainted indictment endeavors.

Simple Snoopy: replying to **Judith** and two others, with the crystal ball saying, "I don't see that happening, that there is going to be training and overhauls in the future – just not needed. All is fair in war with Donald Trump, no love here."

Reply to Witches Stewing Brews of Evil: Is it you, or perhaps the broom used for making those super natural predictions for you? "Oh, tempest in a teapot."

Who are your other two accomplices asking about plotting times?

"When shall we three meet again in thunder, lightning, or rain?" You three are from Macbeth – it's the same famous lines uttered by the three witches planning the next rendezvous for evil.

Not sure whether to call this Jon, who showed up, **Voight, Midnight Cowboy, or the Rock legend,** and decided on the more flamboyant latter. So, as Simple Snoopy, doing my investigative probing, I asked him to explain, "Entertainers must be able to take sides on race or anything else divisive and nasty in political discourse."

No, certainly not what I am saying. They should present both sides as knowledgeable of the entire gamut of issues, but knowledge is a foreign word, so brimful is disliked, and possibly the instructions from their man above in the organization. Oh, I finally got the (Jon) Bon-Jovi thing. Should I be calling you a Thundercat, Simple Snoopyl...Ho! Haha, how absurd.

Simple Snoopy: You are a slow man to get the drift on the Bon Jovi thing. Acquire a wealth of knowledge, since you don't have that and the talent of the real Jon Bon Jovi guy, and you may hate yourself when you even look in the mirror – look enough, it's sure to crack from side to side.

Pay attention Bon-Jovi, it's not finality, as the cases are being argued, while you already have made the ignorant determination to convict. If you think you're the Rock Star Man! Dream on Thunder, Stray Dog, or Alley Cat, no difference what you call me, but seeing your putrid views of hate and lack of worldly knowledge will immediately downgrade you from that revered rock status to that of a cheap entertainer.

You desecrate the name of that Icon! I'm harping on equality unto the law, civilized jurisprudence, sans weaponization and political influence and bias, and for all, including you and me, the equal protection of the law, with ability and recourse to appeal and readdress, especially when as clear as daylight, connivance, plotting, and scheming with every in the unwritten rule of "Get" and prevent Trump from contesting the elections, come hell or high water, from the Atlantic to the Pacific, River to the Sea, and all the ponds in between, because uneasy with ineptness, lies the head that currently wears the crown.

The Changing Tide of Positivity: Jump on Board!

Some remorse seems there for the horrible comments by the deadly anti-Trump mob, when persuasive (cajoling, responding to them in kind) is there after the conversation. Americans, after all, are the Best! Vote for whom you want, but with a conscience, make an informed choice, and see how we have gone backward as a nation over the last few years!

Family values, America first, our own citizens, and charity begins at home. Send money for the wannabe illegals to get a good life in the country where they live! Race, color, and creed don't matter. America does. America the Beautiful is Blessed. Let that not ever change! Act Locally, do good nationally, and create the future globally! It is within you to do this in taking our values, not the future of America and we cannot stumble, fumble, be frail, and fall in cracks and fissures.

We Don't Abandon Allies. But Pay Your Fair Share

Of course, as Lord Nelson said at the Battle of Trafalgar, England expected every man to do his duty during the times of Napolean, as we would expect Donald Trump to as well. Nobody in their right mind would abandon NATO, General, so you be prepared to fight and quit the undisciplined rhetoric that he's the 'mafia type' that 'hates alliances.'

If you know anything about current affairs, NATO is a toothless tiger without the USA, and it cannot be entirely subsidized with American taxpayer money. Economics and not nonsense here - when can people stop thinking along party lines and begin looking at the country's interests, our economics, safety, and then the well-being of the world follows.

NATO is are master in the Art of the Raw Deal. They need to pitch-in, in ratio and proportion to their GDP and the threats they face, equitable and fair in the share – no delinquency in their contribution obligations, in men, money, and motivation! America needs to hold them accountable and not abandon them.

We need to support Europe and NATO members, just as we did many of them in World War II, and commit to a life-long relationship beyond the next four years of the next administration. That promise and commitment reside in the American DNA, and despite the rhetoric of Trump or Biden to any other pro or contrarian views, those are simply election rhetoric.

Nevertheless, while NATO shores up its unity in the wake of the threats to Ukraine, let us not abandon Klitschko, Lomachenko, and Usyk. How about you Rock Stars who will benefit from the publicity made to them with Live Aid Concert for Pain and Suffering?

A country must enjoy independence, from Tibet to the countries in Asia, Europe, and Africa. We will fight any conquest of Australia also, if we find the safety of ACDC, their fight tooth and nail cricket team, Mario L, or Tommy Emmanuel are threatened.

Extremism, integrity and safety of their countries are all priceless in the call to earn their protection from Big Brother, the United States. Donald Trump will, no doubt, follow the advice of his Military Generals, but not the evil rants of the ton of Bull from the Public Sale of the workings of Security by Gone Bolton. His disingenuousness has been exposed in this book and that of other evil doers.

Making Business Sense and Legal Strategy

At every twist and turn, the DT team kept haters and lovers second-guessing. The average and educated individuals, mobs, gangs, armchair critics, and others, however, seem to lack the fundamental knowledge and savviness that business sense and legal strategy have a nexus. You throw the bloodhounds off the trail and scent, and as astute poker players, you never show your hand.

So it is with great dismay that the so-called experts (in their brains) seem outfoxed at every turn of these events. It's still the "Art of the Deal" and is a reason that during the four years of the Trump Presidency, we had no wars; little Rocket Man postured and kept quiet, as did China, Iran, the terrible Taliban, while NATO has only bitched, not paid their fair share.

Imagine the dismay after the gathering of known haters on MSNBC's "The Weekend" before the Monday of, March 25, 2024. It was rejoicing and hysterics on the perceived dilemma the former president faced on the threat to have his assets seized. Running almost in parallel, was a date to be set on that same day for a court for hush money trial. In the end, the option was but with little choice to snuck heads where the sun didn't shine, for you underestimated his ability to overcome, the steely resolve, and your own nothingness stuck out like a sore thumb.

Where is the sense of fair play as human beings? Large sections of Americans were utterly flabbergasted that you would celebrate misfortune and victimization with such public displays by the 'final say' on everything, invariably getting it wrong, hosts Michael Steele, and others. Steele is a known hater of the other side now. Pitiful to see them gloat when, instead, they should express outrage and sympathy for what is happening in the country to everyday Americans. How would he be dumb when he's smarter than the low-life achievers that will languish in side roles on the channel, someone asked.

Chapter 9:
Tales of Ergonomic Faulty Design and Withering Lettuce

Sparring with someone is cordial as, initially, both sides will test the waters to see if there are similar or contrarian views. Once it is established that either it is one sided illogical rant and hatred, with no substantiation, the stupidity in the opposing side of the conversation invariably leads to heated arguments. The emphasis, as stated, is to put things in proper perspective for a morally, ethically, legal, and common-sense educational frame of mind. The abundance of ignorance is, more often than not, appalling, to say the least.

In this encounter, **Freddy (Krueger)** comes along with immediate aggression and no pleasantries. For sure, I thought he was the evil deal from Elm Street. So, with his first unsavory comment, I told him that he had caused enough nightmares there. Krueger showed up on Saturday, March 22, 2024, and proclaimed, "Trump says he has nearly $500M in cash, and the bond wouldn't be a problem at all, and that he could afford bond in New York AG case...." **What changed in this drama now, after all that big talk?**

The judge should look at this closely to see what sort of crooked artistry he was up to, a fast one perhaps? The overseer must verify the source of the cash, when all along he was pleading poverty. Determine exactly where, from the cash, all of a sudden, the $500 million in cash appears. He's been pleading billionaire poverty all week – a miraculous piece of magic.

Simple Snoopy: With all the nonsensical persecution **nightmare causing Fred,** you must be one hateful, pathetic individual. Love and Live Longer, and the reverse is true - choose the latter for health and well-being.

He's lying, nightmare declared. There is no money. He just had to perpetuate the fantasy that he's "really rich" because the evidence that he's a fraud was just revealed!

Simple Snoopy: And if he posts the money on Monday or finds appropriate alternate solutions, then accept that you are the fraud perpetuating nightmares and hate here!

We'll need to exorcise you as you've caused a lifetime of terror on that street and have now crossed geographic boundaries. America must curb these acrimonious and terroristic impetuosities.

Shelia BabyWhich (no problem here, for she called herself a witch, so expected fire, thunder, and rain**):** "You will swear you are the duped and a member of a cult if Trump doesn't post the money Monday."

Simple Snoopy: As an independent, I'd club you with the fraud theory-perpetuating, hate-spewing Bastille mob, duped by their indoctrination. Will urge all to get a deeper understanding of the rule of law, due process, the presumption of innocence, the equal application of law, and unbiased justice, regardless of the mighty, to the poor as the church mouse kind. Whether he pays or not, you and I are not going to get a dime for the limited value of useless conjecture. So, keep the love flowing, and put off the ferocious hate for later or never.

Marilyn Mony: Boy, where did Trumpy all of a sudden come up with that kind of money? Who did he hit up for it? Maybe it just landed in his hand!

Simple Snoopy: Maybe he's selling portraits of you, beautiful Monroe, and some never-before pics with JFK! Why doubt someone's wealth, ingenuity, and resourcefulness – I don't mine, you do likewise or get the smarts.

Ronald President: At Trump's age, I'm still working now more than my co-workers. They all come to me for answers. Sorry, but I also am 77, and there should be term and age limits in place unless that person can prove to be mentally sharp and stable. There are some that do well and much older, but not many, and President Joe, well, he should know that he's had a few drinks with that Parkinson's gait and the stammered speech.

That is an injustice to the country if he is unable to step away – What is his true reason to hang on when the body and mind are sending clear signals to walk away, dumbass?

Simple Snoopy: Mr. Reagan, I'd vote for you any day- Your policies were Excellent and still stand the test of time! Proving your mental acuity and cognition is important. A tribute to you, as loudly as ACDC may say, For Those About to and Still Rock n Rolin - We Salute You.

Yardbird Man: Good thing boomers know everything and don't need any help. Foolish pride has never created problems for anyone.

Simple Snoopy: Clapton, you are speaking way ahead of your generation, man. Regarding the **"Foolish pride,"** your words were the same as Layla's. Nice to have you here, man.

Those lyrics about hiding show basement strategies and false pride will not work in 2024: "What will you do when you get lonely? No one waiting by your side? You've been running, hiding much too long. You know it's just your foolish pride."

KayBush: To me: Hang on Sloppy, you as diabolical as him - DT?

Simple Snoopy: Ok, diabolical? Write a note, wrong key! The Rolling Stones are looking to evil singers, chorusing on their hit Sympathy for the upcoming Goat and Devil concert - would ya care to audition - Big Bucks there. They sing kind of strange and bluesy anyway, so your off-key hollering would be a match made in heaven for the devils and their song.

Chapter 10:
Academic Dishonesty Amidst Political Firestorms

The term copycat, quite unnecessarily gives these wonderful animals a bad name. It is amazing how animals are maligned and humans glorified, with accolades and degrees. Plagiarism is theft, in using the hard work of someone who has worked like a dog, and then this uncool cat steals the work of another and tries to pass it off as his or her own, without acknowledging the work, words or ideas or what that the fancy word for thieving is, i.e. without correct and proper attribution to the original creator.

The steal can be a misdemeanor to a felony, and the chance of getting caught is great with technology. Just heed the advice of Bessie Smith that you've gotta pay yer dues if you wanna sing the blues, and Ringo will tell you that it don't come easy, as you have to burn the midnight oil with the toil. Theft that is not forgiven and forgotten, like any ill-gotten goods.

Conversations on Plagiarism

Joan: Terrible and brazen this whole thing about cheating. First it was Gay, then this Neri Oxman stuff. Did not know she was the wife of Harvard Donor Bill Ackman? She also had no choice but to say she regretted the Plagiarism Allegations. The usual stuff in support, though, is that she is black, and Claudine Gay's resignation as Harvard president is nothing but a racist attack – instead of calling this out for the academic crime it is.

Mary: Will they rescind Neri Oxman's MIT PhD is a good question? Oh, that will be called anti-Semitic, even though it is crystal clear she committed plagiarism and is not entitled to the degree. This sets a bad example again of one group of people exerting their power and wealth to cheat others who have followed the rules and achieved out of merit. Bill Ackman most likely cheated at Harvard as well and needs to have his degree rescinded – will they?

Simple Snoopy: It is a problem, and now the AI tool ChatGPT worsens it, by making it so easy to copy. A degree can also be rescinded years later if detected and academic fraud comes to light. Your university believes that you committed an academic integrity violation. There is no limit on when the university can bring charges; they can open an investigation into the incident – but only if it gets detected. If, during the academic hearing process, you are found willfully or unknowingly responsible for cheating or plagiarism, they can rescind your degree. You cannot plead ignorance.

Non-Plagiaristic Musings: From the Desks of Learned Lewis and Simple Snoopy

We all need to come together, and the divisive forces need to simmer down on all sides. The crooked one-sided view of Morning Joe' is bent to one side, such that you must only watch a re-run at night, for if you do that in the morning, the day will go bad! He Sharpton is every bit as divisive as Hillary's name-calling of Trump supporters and voters and names. So, they are the cultists in Iowa, and the country won't elect an 'Indicted Charlatan.'

By the way, they say Hillary is always waiting in the wings. This was an interesting comment on social media, which said (quoting unedited): Never write Hillary off! She's there trying to sneak in mainly to undo the horny legacy of macho gun-wielding Buffalo Bill mainly, and less about the email cover-up.

Luckily for some limited freedom of speech, people in America can say anything true about current and past Presidents. Now, the Russians don't play second fiddle diddle, and Americans have been granted by Putin the liberty to go and twist and shout this out before the Kremlin! What a great country we are, indeed. Politicians are thick-skinned, and it doesn't hurt Trump, Bush, Clinton, or Obama, just Joe in the polls.

No Supporting Cheating in Academia

He (Sharpton) is the ubiquitous Bait Racer, there in a jiffy, on the scent, at the event, to bait only those who buy the perpetual racial rant when the world wants to come together for America! C'mon, Rev. Al, you cry wolf and racism with every breath you take. From Harvard to the sale of the Holy Bible, inflaming the racial flames is the name of your evil game. Respected Reverend Al, retire this racial stuff, for it is total irreverence to humanity; the way you are doing it now is hurting your credibility with African Americans! America First, Race Second.

This plagiarism is not about race-it's about cheating and getting caught. Ask Dylan, Keller, and a host of others to try to pass off the work of others as their own. Plagiarism is against the grain of ethics and morality and is despicable. All races and people are equal, but not all humans are.

No, it is Not Racism! If a scholar cannot give credit with proper attribution using the institutions' referencing conventions (APA, Harvard, Blue Book, etc.) and lack the skills and adeptness to assimilate, analyze, and then write and present the content in one's own words, with correct academic integrity norms, the concerned person is getting educated beyond their intelligence and cannot expect a Pass for Cheating the World!

The act is unpardonable whether you are the President of Harvard, the USA, or the son of the Libyan President, or any Joe. Plagiarism does not know the color of skin, for the standards of academic honesty only recognize what is there. There are no excuses, and it's a flimsy and false one under the guise and garb of racism, Reverend. Keep to your preaching side of the heavenly lane.

All major plagiarizers should have their degrees rescinded- willful or inadvertent; at that level, it's an academic crime and warrants the stiffest censure and the taking away of all the goodies and titles.

We know that Neri Oxman, the spouse of Harvard mega-donor Bill Ackman, showed some hesitation and kind of offered a remorseful apology after plagiarism allegations surfaced. So, as Simple Snoopy, learning so much from my esteemed colleague.

Learned Lewis: I'd propose a new phrase: People who live in Glass Houses should protect their rear ends, cos, your transgressions are going to come and bite in the Ass! You'd better watch out for AI detection software out there. It is like Santa, who 'gonna find out who's naughty and nice.' It can examine current and past works theses and identify accurately from where you stole your stuff.

So, Reverend, do support the good in America, regardless of race. Keep to the teachings and preachings of religious texts – we are all equal in the eyes of God – Unless the Preacher says otherwise, which is an aberration! We need your help and those of others for a new and better equality for all today and tomorrow.

Has the Sun Set on the Empire?

Tis time to elevate your status and be a leader for all of America and not this one individual, or any. Be open and magnanimous, forget the past and let's change for prosperity, with a Changing of the Old Guard in 2024.

Americans do not need to follow the schedules of the Changing the Guard at Buckingham Palace or the King's Daily change of Guard and underwear. We got our independence from them in 1776 and spilled their tea in disrespect on December 16, 1773.

They say that after all these years, India is going to sue for losses suffered by the East India Company. But we are in good hands with Trump the grizzled veteran in handling lawsuits, who was quite pally with Modi the last time around.

Anyhow, that tea appeasement and damage control has already begun, discreetly and without much fanfare, as United States Ambassador for IT Bill Gates was spotted recently sipping tea from a roadside stall in Hyderabad or somewhere there. Never before has Tea diplomacy been more important than now, with Mr. T heading the government in India. It's no longer just Tea for Two, as envisioned in 1924. Rather, the wonderful progressions of the song are the inspiration for extended racial harmonies and bigger Tea parties! Well, if Scotland gets its Yard to investigate the dwindling sales of its booze, these detectives have it on a T-tray to explain.

Al, so let's not be like the idiotic-lovable Bundy TV character. Instead, 'Be the Change You Want to be in the World,' borrowing from the Great Gandhi – equality for all, not for one race. Let's not wait for leaves to fall or turn brown in any season. We can change starting from late November 2024.

We need unity to get us to a bright future and positive change. No more societal disruptors, just disruptive innovators. Change can be disconcerting and discomforting for the unprepared, uninitiated, or complacent. C'mon, man, offer your support, let the Ole Guard Vamoose!

Chapter 11:
Learned Lewis Recommendations and Reality Check: End the Nightmare!

Learned Lewis is taking over for a few minutes here! Regardless of the outcome of the election in 2024, the view of Snoopy and me is that we all must be united and committed to the success of All in America: White, Black Brown, and even chameleonic. We exhort the current administration not to use race for votes and then let them down, as has happened. Our view is that there is genius in every individual in America. There is a Carl Lewis or a Michael Jordan in each of us in our own way, which we must nurture and allow to blossom.

Positive Change must mean a quantum leap into the future and progress, with leadership that is committed to serving people, and not their political ambitions. On our part, we (wishful thinking maybe) can serve to instill the following 3 critical values. Believe it or not, Simple Snoopy and I have a blueprint for America to:

- Improve education from early childhood to adulthood and maturity.
- Promote the love for the family as a unit through community and social endeavors.
- Transform positively and create a level playing field for all.

No politics here as we must shore up the home base to cater to our own legal citizens/residents, and the world is better for it. As we speak of cognitive decline, we must arrest the decline in education and the increase in foolishness with a top-down and bottom-up strategy. Stemming the alarming declines in mathematics and reading skills requires change and innovation, with the implementation of a Blueprint for Success!

Good Riddance to Bad Idiocy from the top can be decided in November 2024!

The country has been in a rapid downward spiral. From the many conversations presented, the burning question and concern is: How can a confused state of mind run a country? Even a 'kiddo' will tell you.

Country Awaken as we need positive change in 2024 and not the Same Ole. Even if the Same Ole (for the global reader, Ole refers to the current 81-year-old President of the United States, Joseph Robinette Bident) has a basement strategy again, it is returning to even greater desperation; we cannot have such high inflation and a struggle to be 'Livin' for the City' anywhere in America!

The concerns of the Great Mr. Stevie Wonder from way back are now an everyday affair as America needs "love and affection" to be "strong, moving in the right direction," and with the talent we are, good jobs, affording a home, should not be like "a haystack needle" – Positive Change as Memories are not Made of This and not these 4 years of Nightmare, as Dean Martin would agree.

Building Blocks of Human Development

Our blueprint, or that of the caring, is to lay the foundation to build Math and Reading skills, which are the building blocks and foundations for the progress of America! These are quintessential competencies and skills vital in everyday life and for successful careers in science, technology, medicine, and engagement in the pursuit of discovery and invention.

The foundations of reading and math must be strongly laid in the formative years of school education through innovative teaching pedagogies; however, the declining standard in both areas suggests failures to achieve this, which is attributed to a multiplicity of reasons. Bad policies must be reversed, and not vote buying by waiving student debt for some. The United States, for all its vaunted economic leadership position, may be severely lagging behind the world in smarts with the invasion we face from land, sea, air and balloon, and retard minds.

While the decline is widespread, data shows it is perhaps more pronounced in the vast majority of minority students. The immediate address of this very dire and challenging situation is imperative to prevent erosion of our leadership in the world and among communities of advanced nations and, importantly, to offer hope and aspiration to US students for the empowerment a quality education provides. Snoopy and Lewis will be pleased to engage and advise for positive Change post-November 2024 for the betterment of America.

A Multifaceted Approach, Not Underachieving Staid and Sedate Policies!

Learned Lewis and Simple Snoopy have found that commitment is required to understand which human-centric solutions are vital to bridge deficits and charter a course of positive inclusiveness for all sections of society.

The dire need of the hour is, therefore, for practical solutions for our future generations while simultaneously improving law, order, and safety in all cities – the chaos we need to hold Joe for, no other. The DAs in certain cities should be trained in enforcing the law, as people are calling for reform and quality.

A multifaceted approach will entail the leveraging of human and adaptive technology integration for personalized learning tailored to individual learning styles. Included will be educational apps, online platforms, and virtual simulations to revolutionize student engagement with mathematical concepts, and reading development.

Analysis and Need for Change

It is amazing that one party has been making promises for years, but the success of minorities has not improved. Change is needed. American need to opt for new and change, and not old, aging, stale and lies.

The alarming data from the National Assessment of Educational Progress calls for drastic action. The lowest in decades in reading and math scores were even more pronounced among Black and

Latino students, English learners, and students from low-income backgrounds experiencing the brunt of pandemic-related upheavals and uncertainties.

The implementation of the findings of our research integrated into a reinforced Blueprint will ensure a new beginning in addressing declining math and reading skills in all American students. The astute implementation holds the promise for a better tomorrow for our most precious resource, our future and hope, children and youth in the United States! Trump realizes this and is an advocate for positive change, we believe.

Racism by the Fakers of Equitable Practices

The shocking and recent deaths of George Floyd and Breonna Taylor have caused lawmakers and corporations to enact equality initiatives in corporations. However, affirmative action reforms have faced difficulties. In a changing world order, in the United States and globally, many employers acknowledge they are duty-bound to ensure a harmonious, equitable, and safe work environment which is devoid of any form of discrimination, harassment, and intimidation.

Although easier said than done, achieving this equality needs a systematic approach to the investigative process of research in an organization, with auditing, mapping, and diagnosing the ills that constrain good and equality practices in academic and professional life.

All going great guns, then reverse Diversity, Equity, and Inclusion (DEI) raises its ugly head with the Rona MacDaniel hiring and firing. Former RNC chair Ronna McDaniel was fired by NBC barely a few days after hire, with intense hate backlash. How can these pseudo advocates Scarborough, Brzezinski, Psaki, Wallace, Reid, O'Donnell and Mad Doe brazenly spout equity day in and day out when they are anti-American, really? It typifies the ignorance of the rule of law, something that is in the appeals process, or moving in that direction, let the courts decide, not the spewers of hate.

The winds of change from the 2021 racial disharmony, protests, and turmoil are already having an impact and have influenced steadfast commitment and improvements for more equitable HR, legal, and organizational approaches. Newer practices are oriented toward enhancing equality overall. Individuals from diverse backgrounds can also proffer actions to further diversity, equity, and inclusion. The aim must be to serve Americans of all races in advancing life, liberty, freedom and happiness while contributing to employment, and improving the quality of life, which has declined over the last few years.

Change for a Better Tomorrow: November 2024 to Fix the Problem

The continued persistence of inequalities is directly the result of divisive policies. Deliberately using race as pawns – look no further than how Bragg, Letitia James, Willis and others are prime examples of manipulation. The American people are intelligent and discerning and will make the right decisions in 2024, for sure.

The incredible talent of the American people must not be abused for personal political mileage and gain. Human-centric solutions are also vital to bridge deficits and charter a course of positive inclusiveness for all sections of society. The urgent need of the hour is, therefore, for practical solutions, for despite well-intended US laws and mandates, some are ignored, set aside by pressures and vested interests, including personal aims and ambitions, and to make the policies of Trump look bad.

But that was foolish, as what matters most to the common folk are the cost of groceries, gas, home, or plainly speaking, food, education, clothing and shelter, and a decent standard of living, all elusive now with policies that are dismal and far from satisfactory.

Fatigued and Tired, Losing Step, Yet Damagingly Lingering On

Hiding in the basement and not showing up in disasters, like the recent chemical one in East Palestine a year after the chemical spill, for that devastating train derailment poses the question – was he afraid the noxious fumes would get to him? Meanwhile, the fumes of his machinations were obvious, he went to Pennsylvania, as the scheming sent Trump to trial. **How convenient, How Evil!**

An East Palestine mother's message to Biden: "Don't use my village as a campaign stop, just help me find a new home" – how gut-wrenching and sad! The Union Carbide caused disaster in Bhopal, India, in December 1984 was a lesson in prompt attention by government officials. The hazardous chemical cocktail spillage needed a visit immediately and not a year later as a campaign damage control and appeasement strategy, Joseph Biden.

All this means you care for yourself and yourself alone and two hoots for others and the country. All of America has seen selfishness! America loses nothing for positive change to replace 50 years of nothingness in public life and false promises that do not uplift society but only elevate personal economic standings! Many are looking at the positives of the Trump Presidency, wistfully and dejectedly at the sad state of the current mob, yearning for better days ahead with his return in 2025.

We need precise solutions to bring about positive social change. The nation needs a skilled and scientific approach to level the opportunity field, which is vital in a country that is truly the recipient of the Almighty's bountiful blessings, which politicians plunder from.

The fatigue has set in the less than four years of old Joe, and his rule, relentlessly divisive and weaponized, falling short of its genuinely demonstrable intent, inevitably sets in, as the lack of progress in visible results is the lament of many. The exhortation by organizational management practitioners and those on the theoretical side of the aisle is for immediate action. America is ready for positive change and good leadership will step up to the plate, with people having genuine reasons for a better future.

Chapter 12:
Off on Haley's Comet!

We all may know that Nimarata Nikki Haley (née Randhawa; born January 20, 1972) is an American politician and diplomat. She first served as the 116th. Governor of South Carolina from 2011 to 2017 and later as the 29th U.S. ambassador to the United Nations from January 2017 to December 2018. At the recommendation of President Donald Trump, Haley became the United States Ambassador to the United Nations.

Haley had a good run in attempting to be the Republican nominee/candidate, but the ingratitude of not dropping out earlier and waiting for bad things to befall the former President and future likely President shows us what politicians are made of and sets aside the image of scoundrels as males only perhaps, to put it mildly. Before Haley dropped out, there were plenty of positives in social circles. Doing my journalistic beat, here are some of the comments on the saga of Nikki Haley.

Indian Election Interference: One

I call this Indian Election Interference because I found a couple on social media pretending to be in India although are in the United States. We'd pardon their lack of fully assimilating into American culture, and perhaps their exposure to American slang and flowery language will hasten this. They blossomed into their true selves with their hidden personalities emerging, as you will see, but needed to be provoked to get going and were followers and not leaders in the discourse.

Cincinnati Cyn: Sinful Cyn from Cincinnati started the ball rolling in this area; Haley wants it both ways, that' the reason she's not doing any better than she is. Folks who want to support her see that she is still holding back and not all in. The attacks she FINALLY made on Trump came way too late. I could handle a Republican President, just NEVER Donald Trump.

Neha: Agree; as someone in India, I'm following this very closely and will say no more to Trump and his scamming family members! The Indian election interference was accompanied by ills about morality in America, their corrupting the world, and that for Neha, Haley, an Indian, would pardon Trump if convicted, was treachery to civilization, to India and the world. She said: "Remove him, and Time to move forward."

Simple Snoopy: What about Joe and his family members? Do you see them as quaky clean like Scrooge McDuck? Now look at the portrait of a jealous Indian woman who cannot bear to see the success of Indian origin, Nikki Haley – she said, "Haley is either threatened by Trump or she is playing both sides and making a fool of the American public, from what we can see in India. The guy cannot be on the ballot and should be in prison, but he is out and about like no laws apply to him."

By the way, naughty Neha, don't try and sneak in across the border - We'll catch and Release in Timbuktu!

Neha: Maybe you are jealous that your wife liked another man's comment more than yours. Is that what triggered you? See, you are wrong in your assumptions that I am who you think I am on all counts. That goes to show you that you cannot believe everything you see on any social media, including news. No, that I've made my comments; you'll research me and go after me.

Simple Snoopy: Look now that you unnecessarily mentioned my wife, I'll say, look at this narrow-minded, jealous woman of hate. Got caught in spewing rubbish and said, "Your wife liked another man's comment more. Quit yer sleeping around - Neha. No one is interested in researching trash-Jealous individual like you. Stay outta America – Prime Minister Modi will be told you are interfering in US elections."

Neha: See here you are so wrong again. I actually voted for Nikki, but see she is wasting my vote when she is making a comment that she wants to pardon your ring leader. Now, that just doesn't sit well with me. Do you understand? Too bad if you don't, you cannot educate all the idiots in America.

Simple Snoopy: Oh, now you are saying you are in America, and were pretending earlier you were in India. Get the F out of here, hate-mongrel! Election interference will be Reported to the FBI and Indian counterparts, ignorant twitch of a B! My apologies, but she crossed the red line with the your wife's comment.

Stop pretending to be jealous of Haley Neha - change the stinking mindset and clothes. You hate Mericans - why are you here - for prosperity? We do not interfere in the elections in India. They are allies. You are the odd woman out and truly a disgrace to the community and India.

International Election Interference: Two

Believe it or Not! There are slime bags here and outside the country interfering in our elections.

Indira: Pretended like Neha, that she was writing all the nasty stuff from overseas.

Response: Simple to get disclosure and get rid of the disguise. Called her Gandhi Girl! She angrily retorted, "You ignorant Americans think that anyone with the name Indira is a Gandhi. "

She started off on the wrong foot by calling the former President a rapist and all supporters in the USA the same – which was just out of bounds. Speaking in such horrible terms about an American President, whether Trump or Biden and Americans, is simply unacceptable. So, a filthy mouth receives similarly in kind. Indira was warned (in jest, of course) of being tracked down by the FBI and the Indian law enforcement internationally.

Simple Snoopy Reply: You are very willfully commenting about allegations in civil trials for which there is no evidence - like the Jean Carrol case - how about you? There may be allegations of all kinds against you, such as pedophilia, desertion of your husband, and raping young boys, and is it Men to Boys?

Super Ignoramus stay out of American-politics-with-hate speech, fake Indira-Gandhi girl, a profound-disgrace to Indians. The real Indira Gandhi was gracious, charming, and noble, as are all or most Indians. Ignorant women with one foot in America and another in India stay out of American politics with hate speech. By the way, we suspect you are the Gislaine Maxwell of India and are under investigation. That put paid to the conversation. I'm sure we will never be bothered again by this fake Indira – a disgrace to the wonderful country of India. **Dotting the I's and Crossing the T's**

Learned Lewis: Haley, for many, is the US reincarnation of Indira Gandhi. She's got the nose, the savviness and nastiness about her, all rolled in one – they say. I do not believe, however, that she can hold a candle to the great Indira Gandhi and now her granddaughter Priyanka – No way, Haley, you are not anywhere close and will never be!

A true leader, but a spoiler, not knowing when to call it a day and say quits from the race. Later on, her true colors showed through her comments to you, SS. You handled it with your typical - commensurate 'give back better than you get.' Surprising that we found extreme hate from Indian-origin ladies in the USA for Haley and Vivek. We took it that there could be two reasons for the possible negativity:

1) Pure jealousy, as inherently, Indians typically take joy in the miseries of their own, and not success.
2) Plenty of hate for Americans, but coming here is fashionable and desirable.
3) Petty, think otherwise. Forget the caste stuff, which is prevalent even here, but there is a different form of racism within the Indian community of North and South Indian origins and other differences.

The caste system is very prevalent in the US and Canada, within and among Hindus, who, in turn, discriminate against other religions and other Americans. School districts and workplaces have banned caste racism in some provinces in Canada and the USA, and now there's legislation as well.

Dot Indians, as opposed to Feather Indians, is the common terminology used by many to differentiate the mistake made by Columbus or Amerigo Vespucci. My theory is that weary with a long voyage and after one too many, Columbus couldn't think straight (like our Guy, who doesn't need intoxicants but is always in a clueless state of euphoria) and thought he had reached Asia, his desired destination. Mistakes do happen – made by Christopher Columbus once then, but by Joe, every day the sone rises!

By the way, the State of the Union address by the president on March 07, 2024, saw a different person speaking. Aggressive, animated, and stimulated is the conclusion of many in America, on the uncharacteristic less error-riddled delivery. To that State of the Union address, Donald Trump found that strange, as normally Biden "can't put together two sentences in a row, he must have been "high as a kite." Trump demanding that Biden be drug tested before next month's debate is a valid requirement.

Amnesia, Dementia, and Plainly, Just Losing It, but Profit Smarts Excellent

One can excuse Columbus for that mistake, and that Indian name never did sit well with Chief Sitting Bull or Tonto, and even Silver; the Lone Ranger's fleet-footed great white stallion gave it a nod of disapproval as well. But Joe, c'mon man, with faxes, GPS, tele and human prompters, you are still as confused as ever. Some facts and fiction for readers. Here are the comparisons from you to separate more Truth and less Lies:

1) U.S. President Joe Biden confused Emmanuel Macron, the current French president, with François Mitterrand, who died in 1996, calling him from Germany and then France. Far worse than Columbus, who can be excused, with no access to record and cassette players, just bugles, trumpets and the Howlin of high winds.

2) His slip was also showing (Carville, what would you say?) when the 81-year-old U.S. president, in July 2023, adept at cover-ups and making things rosier than the actual dismal state, said "over 100" Americans have died from COVID-19 since the pandemic broke out."

The specially assigned damage control staff that follow him around like faithful puppies, infuriated Commander, who in fits rages of jealousy, went on biting sprees, although on far less scale than how those with the bigger canines sink their teeth, molars and dentures into the weaponized targets, unlike the innocent big pooch. The White House later corrected this to "over 1 million."

Poor Commander got the axe and the raw end of the stick, while the more savage is elevated and rewarded for the good assistance provided, which includes the following **Please Help Me, I'm Falling Strategies**: Curb & Roadside Assistance 24-7, Stair and Step Ladder distance minimizers, camera lenses mandatorily covered to prevent the capture of stumbles and 'hot mike' and cuss words, and AI changing stumbles, to athletic Bob Beamon leaps and more.

Columbus also downplayed and kept mum the decimation of 95 percent of the indigenous populations following European colonization, amounting to an estimated 20 million people. Our conclusion is that both are masters of deception.

1) **Head I win, tales you lose**: No profits are parted with outside the clan. Columbus, on the other hand, was held accountable for all spears, arrows, totem poles and gold brought in by Ferdinand II and Isabella I, the Catholic Monarchs of Aragon, Castile, and Leon in Spain.

Columbus can be cut some slack in confusing America with India due to any of the possibilities of insobriety. Scurvy or real Indians disguised, knowing in advance of his landing, with their advanced skills in mathematics and fortune telling, that America would one day be the World's Greatest trading post in the future.

2) In June 2024, mass confusion in calling the war in Ukraine with that in Iraq. Joe said that Russian President Vladimir Putin was "losing the war in Iraq. He's losing the war at home, and he has become a bit of a pariah around the world," Difficult to say if he meant Saddam Hussein losing the war in Ukraine as well.

3) **Our Advice and Recommendation**: We offer here a couple of strategic recommendations (in bold) regarding Joe to the Joint Chiefs of Staff from fact and fiction but for the good of the country.

   a) **Taking a page out of 'MAD and Spy Vs Spy, many foreign leaders like Rocket Man and Putin have doubles to confuse the already confused Joe. Here is a suggestion given to Joe:**

   Our advice is to have your own doubles, with yourself (the real you) branded like cattle ranchers do, with your secure brand that nobody can peddle. The identity branding will be a safeguard to ensure you are not confused with the double and do not send the double as you to international and major domestic events. Leaders and people will notice if the double speaks without a fumble, and the game will be over.

   b) **Provide daily geography and history lessons in the morning on the locations of Canada, Mexico, and World countries, and fundamentals on economics, so he correctly sees the decline in consumer confidence.**

   With you being more fluent in obscenities than gentlemanly language, it was distressing how belligerently and insultingly you reportedly spoke to the Canadian Prime Minister with faulty personal intelligence. Thinking that the hordes of illegal immigrants pouring into the country were from Canada.

   The three conversations were picked up in the USA by several planted Russian moles, Chinese listening posts on farmlands and nuclear installation in the US, and TikTok, as the following internal commands issued by Joe:

   Get the S.O.B. Trudeau. While he should be getting double pneumonia from our economic coughing and spluttering, the moron wants to take our wealth. I'm hearing he's planning an invasion of the United States, with an amphibious assault on the beaches of the US side of the Great Lakes called Operation Dumkirk! We already have Trump, and you'll be next.

   This is the real conspiracy and insurrection and both your names start with 'Tru' – irrefutable proof, there itself that will shut the traps of the Supreme Court. Quick, we'd get word on Truth Social and Fakebook before they censor me, rambling about me. Prepare to deploy and activate regular and reserve components of the Army Reserve and Army National Guard in all strategic locations to keep them out.

   I'm not sure if it's my imagination, but I feel the earth tumbling down as the walls seem to be shaking and the earth quaking, its Carole King meets ACDC. It is just age or me, as I seem to be less than a quarter of the man I once was; I need to reach out to the real number one running the show for help! Oh, Barak, Barak, Where Art Thou? Whither Thou Goest I Will Go! Oh Boy, I love listening to Mahalia and Michael Jackson.

Invasion I: The Russians Aren't Coming, Britt Revenge & the Indians have Arrived.

The Russians aren't coming, as their Yellow Submarine was easily spotted near Connecticut, and neutralized by placing a sandbar there to run them aground, no Nukes, just Environmentally friendly strategy.

Connecticut, meanwhile, isn't all that innocent. They sent someone even before Columbus got here to infiltrate and mess up the Knights of King Arthur's Round and Merlin's magic sometime in the late 5th and early 6th centuries. Rumor has it that Britain has never forgotten and has vowed vengeance.

UK's Secret Intelligence Service - also known as MI6, has recruited the services of Mr. Atkinson Bean to come to America during the confusion of the November elections and abduct Entebbe, or Adolf Eichman style, some high-profile US politicians like UN Ambassador Girl, Utah man, Bridge man, Tuppence, Pencil Neck, Insider Trader Lady, Shuscheemer, etc. Little do they know, our security would not lift a finger and say good riddance.

This time, the boat will be equipped with GPS to go around Icebergs and will have the capacity for weighty cargo to haul back! The ship captain has reassured a nervous Mr. Bean that it would be truly unsinkable this time around and to just sing My Heart Will Go On during the missionit **Stinks but Always Floats and Never Sinks**!

But now the Indians have arrived! The good ones are contributing to the USA. The bad ones are invading India. Watch out for the bad ones. They are a tricky lot! Plenty of fake calls using Voice Over Internet Protocol (VOIP) from India, using fake Indian names like George, Steve, Stella Starlight, John Smith, Sweet Lady Jane, etc., but betrayed by their outrageously faked American accents and horrendous Grammar. One fakey tried Quincy Jones but didn't have his cues right!

They think New York is the capital, but now that will change with the Trump case and the mentally stunted Ergonomic and Lettuce thievery. New York cries out, "What Have They Done to My Song Ma," which could be well its story and for Melanie and Miley to redo for the city.

Usually preying on Seniors job seekers, claiming to be from the IRS, and into identity theft, bank accounts and much more, which would make Swiper from Dora feel like a saintly Fox.

Invasion II: The Chinese Invasion & Hoodwinking the Hoods

This is real Smart Spy vs Stupid Spy stuff going on between the USA and China. Only the cunning of Simple Snoopy on a mission has been able to be the Master Spy, match wits and scoop this out from the trenches of international intrigue and deceit.

The Chinese are not at all bothered that we punctured their ballon. They are unafraid of Joe because they can see the fake spring in his step when in public and the aircraft carrier-like turns and pivots. They anticipate a response of Joe sending a Slow Boat to China, which they will counter more easily than we did, as it took us months with their kite(s).

The purpose of the balloon was, of course, very strategic in gathering all military secrets, close to all their properties in the US first, and then others. They also took a census of the herds of sheep, cattle and idiots and know exactly who's who, from top – down. Less interested from the bottom up because they believe if you get the head to tumble, the body will grumble but then eventually crumble.

Their intention is to confuse the confused with real Ying Yang. Our Learned friend translated, that Ying Yang means retaliate with God and Devil, Sin and Grace, Action and Passion - **How appropriate to trick the Axle of Evil and the head**.

Now, we all know that the Chinese are smart and cunning; they built all their weaponry and technology by cloning the technology of, they say, with a snicker, US clowns. They have said that President Xi Jinping will deal only directly with President Joe.

When two great leaders were introduced to each other, in formal gun salutes and ceremonial pleasantries, Joe didn't take a step backwards (fearing he'd fall), and he thought President Xi Jinping was calling himself the Kingpin of China. Joe promptly told him that he was the Kingpin of the USA!

Now, in the important "Show Me the Money" conversation, President Xi let our "Big Guy" know that he would make all payments in multiple currencies of Yuan (China), Yen (Japan), and Won (Korea). This set off huge concerns in the administration on how would the King in his Parlor be counting all his Yuan, Yen, and Won - Money, in an already bewildered and confused state?

This was a ploy by the crafty Chinese to introduce three currencies to Joe at one time and achieve the aim of China, the Mullahs in Iran and others to hasten the De-dollarization and the world's reliance on the U.S. dollar (USD) as the chief reserve currency.

Look, Joe, what is happening under your reign? Wars, inflation, international loss in our pride, and if the Chinese take over the world, no mercy, it will be a slavery of Americans. They are cruel and brutal! No dogs and cats and the SPCA will be shuttered.

There is some hope, however, in hoodwinking them. They are trying to steal the technology we used in their mind to get Di Caprio's DNA from the Titanic and clone him for real life. Let's play along, invite their students and earn the Yuan that these Universities clamor for foreign students from China. We can furtively infect their computers with bugs that will mess up scientific formulas and show our tent cities as tourist spots. A combination of Stealth and Shock treatment, the Chinese may even sell back our land in a distress sale, and presto! The Fentanyl crisis is over.

The Real Upstarts

The Universities and America have learned that the liberal professors are also behind some of the stealing of secrets, and Death to America calls for their anti-American and socialist leanings preached in class. No question, they have a hand; this learned lot has contributed through ignorance to the pillage and plunder of our intellectual and worldly properties. We need to Smarten up at the Top, the bottom is smart but is called horrible names.

A former president who knows business needs to be acknowledged for those skills. He quieted Soleimani, and he strengthened the bonds of rocket friendship between Sir Elton John and Kim, has built-in Pune, India, while they (conmen from India, scam the elderly and prey on the gullible) steal here and countless other ways. Iron Mike may be assigned to handle those who say otherwise.

You must Abdicate the Throne! America will give you a Parlor and even get the government to legally get some of the gold from McKenna, and Sen. Bob Menendez, to you. We will also petition the government for you to be in the lap of luxury, with Julius and Queen Cleopatra-style milk baths to defy the aging process. You just set your terms, Simple: Ask and Thou shall Receive.

Disingenuous Reasons in Praise for Haley

Learned Lewis: The amazing jealousy and hate for Donald Trump are the result of party influence, indoctrination, and not independent studied smarts. We would like to see people look at both sides of the coin, but that's wishful stinking of such a possibility. The fake praise lavished on Haley by many was more in the remote hope she'd replace Trump as the nominee and then be defeated by Biden – Haley was not smart enough to see this though. Now in May 2024, perhaps ant act of contrition, has come around and will be supporting Trump.

It is really fear of DT, for reluctantly, grudgingly, and inwardly, many know that he is a force to be reckoned with. Some admit that the country was far better off earlier. Over to Snoopy's Both Sides Now "Sparks Fly – Spar and Bickering Encounters of the Third (turd) and dirty kind, which are revelations and also highly educational, I must admit and gives me an opportunity to put in the finishing touches, where possible. Go Simple Snoopy for America!

This gent's name is Amundsen South Pole Scott: Reporting from there, he said: Haley, to beat Trump, you must be vicious and bring up Trump's weaknesses to the public. Haley needs to outline her strengths, but alas, although it's been a meteoric rise, I think she introspectively realised her own ingratitude to him, and she cannot be VP now played on her mind, although she'll never admit this.

In the end, it was an ignominious exit that showed her true colors of personal ambition over any semblance of loyalty, which is not good for party and politics. She just faltered for Trump to win without mounting any political challenge. Haley will be honorably mentioned in history as the person who ineptly allowed Trump to win the 2024 GOP nomination.

Simple Snoopy: Amundsen, stop preaching viciousness, man, keep the shrill of hate thrill, confined to the chill of the South Pole! It's people like you that are creating mayhem, hate, and pitting Americans against each other. Speak of love for fellow humans, and not instigation and trouble-mongering. Poor DT is overcoming adversity in style - salute such bravery against the odds and decry the sustained persecution!

Simple Snoopy: A friend said, I was so sure that she was going to win, otherwise would have gone to his camp and told them to spread the news that she was born in Punjab, India, as he (Trump) did with Obama. This thought made sense and came to me, he said, after watching an old movie of Peter Sellers and Sophia Loren, and the song line: "I remember that with one jab of my needle in the Punjab, How I cleared up beriberi, And the dreaded dysentery.

Learned Lewis: Oh, you are talking about the Millionaires from around 1960, But it was the start of bigger things, as George Martin, the famed late Beatles' producer – arranged for the song to be recorded for the soundtrack of the film The Millionaires. Well, that is the precursor to great things for Martin, the Beatles, and the lovable Inspector Clouseau (Snoopy, you remind me of him, but you are way nastier), and of course, Loren and Ponti had wonderful careers – next for Trump, going by the mess we are in.

By the way, SS, I love the theme song from The Pink Panther, and my favorite is to improvise playing it on the Piano. In fact, all the kitty songs, like Alley Cat, have that lilting mischievous air about them, which lifts spirits and makes us appreciate nature, cats and all animals on earth, and Donald Trump, if I may add – ha ha!

Simple Snoopy: As said before, Haley is the US reincarnation of Indira Gandhi! She's got the nose, the savviness and the nastiness about her all rolled in one! I'm saying this under my breath, for I do not know how the other side would take it, and if it gets to her walkathon Grandson in India – I am talking about the Indira political tribe! But back to business, and here are some vile Americans discussing things.

Note from SS: Not sure if this was the Killing Me Softly Lady in this forum, but she pretty much achieved the same effect with the Song here:

R. Flack and Friends: 1. Very proud of this lady Haley, whether she wins or not - has the guts to give it back to him. 2. She is a truly brave lady, proud of her, and has swatted her house twice and she keeps going. 3. She's been pulling punches this entire primary, refusing to directly condemn Trump for his obvious criminal activity because she's trying to walk the line of not fully alienating all of the MAGA cult - I can only assume with the possibility his legal cases will eventually derail his campaign.

Learned Lewis: Can't help myself, but the repeated reference to "Lady" gets me nostalgic about the icons and fine gentlemen: Kenny and Lionel – ok, time to move on!

Fury: I'm a lifelong conservative and definitely will vote for Nikki and not DT. And would even have held **my nose** and voted for Biden over him. Wishing her luck, and while I am even talking to make a little donation for her.

Lodger Roger: I like her as well, Fury. I was born into being a Democrat but am now registered as an independent. I vote for the person and Nikki is a consideration in the general election. I gave $10.00 to her campaign this month. It's not much, but I will try and do it each month she is in this. If we all do a little something it goes a long way.

Simple Snoopy: Fury, blow the snot out of your nose instead of holding it up, though, man! Hope you're not the Tyson boxer guy; it cost you'd come and beat me up! Well, nice to see you parting with the dinero Shylock-Lodger Rodger. You publicize meagerly good deeds well! However, this is all kind of fake, that you would vote for Haley, with all the buts and ifs, as she will depart the stage ingloriously soon, is my prediction. This election is going to be decided by economics, immigration, the safety of Americans, and our future, for which Biden has performed dismally.

Bill Cracken: Nikki's strategy is to avoid saying anything bad about Trump (i.e. his 91 felony charges, lies, disparaging remarks, racism, authoritarian aspirations, etc.) for fear of losing any trump supporters. Why would you vote for Haley when she won't call out her leading GOP opponent?

Simple Snoopy: Nikki is a goner sooner rather than later. Somebody needs to tell her to drop out as it is an exercise in futility, and she will drop when she sees there's a greater chance of an iceberg in the Sahara than inching any way forward! That's how my wisdom played out! She dropped out, was getting nowhere and now realizing her forlly, will be voring Trumpover catastrophic Biden,

Jingle Jangle: Small Hands Donald Trump, well, his criminality stuff starts to hit the fan with multiple felony trials. She won't be there as a much smarter and logical alternative than an extremely flawed GOP candidate who was going to go down in flames in the general election! You know, as well as I know, that Haley does not have a chance in hell at beating Biden I think she is only trying to help him.

Simple Snoopy: Jingle-Jangle, you calling him 'Small Hands is funny, for he is 6'4", and one finger would be sufficient to squeeze your manly Jingle Jangles, and you'd be singing soprano better than Kenny G's embellished and jazz-inflected Sax runs. You are the smart but obnoxious kind - the man with da-wisdom teeth intact amidst the dentures. Knowing you, if a denture went down your throat, you'd reuse it!

Chapter 13:
A Goddess on a Mountain Top: Venus

The "odor of mendacity" (attribution Judge, Scott McAfee) still menacingly hovers and lingers, with a lot of other legal paraphernalia and stench, with likely negative fallout on the career, future, and efforts of the over-zealous prosecutor, Fani Willis.

The odor of mendacity meant that the entire process stinks to glory if ever such a thing is possible. The judge was smart and tried to be politically correct without directly saying this is going nowhere; he did do so in an indirect way using a stink bomb, as powerful as the one dropped in Hiroshima in the stink and not radioactive terms!

Civilized and Not-so in Mid-March, 2024: The Verdict on Evil

A local prosecutor who is charging a former president with election interference is unprecedented in the annals of American case law and history. In a close election, as a matter of wanting to know more,

Trump has a legitimate claim of immunity. He is immune from being prosecuted for actions he took while he was still president. Some overhauls of our laws are bound to be in the works in the future, for a businessman entering the sphere of politics has exposed the inadequacies of the legal system perpetrated by and from the Axle of Evil!

Learned Lewis on Human Aspirations and Frailties

In the company of Simple Snoopy, his sense of humor is rubbing off on me. I'm not monkeying around when I say that Fani Willis (whom Snoopy calls Venus Willis) was a Daydream Believer. I'm guessing that taking in the dizzying possibility of fame and the illusions of glamor, being called a rising star in the field of law, she saw charging a former President of the United States as a ticket to superstardom. Grandeur, by how incredibly rosy the future would look like, but alas, it was not meant to be, the way this should all play out.

Little choice but to save face where it was started, rather belated as their framing is falling apart in their stated Fani Willis 'Inconsistencies, the after-the-fact discovered by the Department of Justice, in a report on Apr 10, 2024. Let me qualify my monkeying around, is to give credit (although I'm not a Harvard man, I know how to do this) to Stewart, who wrote the song and the Monkeys.

Borrowing from Wikipedia (more reliable now than before), Stewart noted that that song was about relationships, where at the start, "both parties are in an idealistic haze, but later artifice falls away and easier confronted with their real selves. Thus, it's this point where love is really proven." Which simply means, coming together for the plot and trickery, getting caught, but life goes on, with the blessings of humanity, for hopefully their love blossoms to more than plotting on many one-night stands!

The First Amendment Protection: Valid and Compelling

The First Amendment protects freedom of speech. The attorneys for Trump have argued that the indictment should be dismissed because the former president's political speech is protected by the First Amendment. Trump contends that his statements about the Georgia results are protected by the First Amendment, with no criminal intent because he genuinely believed he won the election.

Why should credence not be given to that clear-as-pure water assertion? In sporting events or in awards that are judged, the losing side may have a different opinion on the final outcome from genuine feelings that could stem from a variety of reasons, and this is no different in Georgia. The term in major sporting events, where the outrageous decisions are sometimes by millions of viewers, is 'robbed' of a draw or victory.

Much water has flowed since when are a motion was filed in late 2023 before the unsuccessful efforts by the defendants to disqualify Willis from the case emerged. Trump's attorney, Steve Sadow, had argued that what transpired during the 2020 presidential election was expected as a part of political speech, calling the indictment problematic.

The other side labelled this as the peddling of conspiracy theories and denounced the claims of widespread voter fraud. But that is politics, where the actions of one political side are disparaged vehemently as a violation. With the flaring of tempers in a close election, the greater power rests with the party with the greater strength. However, the methods to dominate politically have been with the meanest means to prevent any future strength in the contest, which is a terrible violation of justice and democracy.

Georgia, No Peace with Deceitful Policial Maneuvering

The passion of Ray Charles in his inimitable rendition of 'Georgia on My Mind' has been possibly shattered, and that vision supplanted in the mind by the discordant and inharmonious shattering of the peace and serenity conveyed by the masterpiece and substituted with horror in the legal contrivance of the lowest manipulative scheming possible.

C'mon, man, stay out of music and timeless themes of American masterpieces and evergreens! Nevertheless, it's not too late to take singing lessons, and it is possible to teach an old dog new tricks; just don't sign in public as you'd forget your lines, but practice and you could be the new, old blue eyes.

Some bickeringly analytical conversations and the stories below tell it all.

The View of Noah, the Ark Man: Although true, Willis showed rather poor judgement; nevertheless, the allegations against Trump and his co-defendants remain unchanged. It's not the conduct of personal conduct and demeanor of Willis, which is irrelevant to the findings. One way to look at it? Equally valid is to see that the First Amendment guarantees the right of expression and freedom of speech.

Simple Snoopy Response: Oh, Noah, you need to focus on herding all the animals to safety before the next apocalypse! Here, you are out of your depth in the understanding of, firstly, the First Amendment, but then the notions of legal jurisprudence and how deceitfully morality and ethics were waylaid. Prosecutorial misconduct and a multitude of improprieties confound how personal ambition brings in cunning to a degree of manipulation never seen before – A New Low!

The intrusion of sexual relationships into a partnership of manipulation was luckily caught on time – imagine if it was not. Disbarment would be a mild penalty for the conduct of errant judicial officials. Ark Man, You need to focus on negotiating the rapids, turbulence, and deep waters and keep the animals safe.

Noah the Ark Man: Are you a Christian religious fanatic or a comedian? I can't decipher where you fall within that spectrum.

Simple Snoopy: That's the problem - trying to decipher religious persuasions, a lack thereof, etc., being judgmental, maligning, vilifying DT, and many others. On the spectrum of biased nonsense, your limited knowledge of the unbridled application of the unbiased law appears missing and faulty. Keep to the rescue mission, O savior of the animals on the planet of lying apes, since you cannot see the malicious and vile conduct of Venus Willis and Wee Willie Wonka Wade.

Denise Roussos: She jumped into the fray with a vengeance in Replying to Simple Snoopy: "Speaking of missing and faulty, the big words are really tripping you up. Hilarious condescension, make-believe intelligent but barely literate."

Simple Snoopy: Replying to Roussos: Roussos, you happen to be tripping with the wrong person in the domains of vocabulary, law, grammar, critical thinking, the arts, and sciences. Will buy yer cheap and sell at a loss! Please produce your Grecian educational transcripts for evaluation in America.

Expand your vocabulary. A new word for deceitfulness for you is mendaciousness (the odor of that word makes it a must for more frequent use of it and its different grammatical uses, which also exemplifies your sheer nothingness in law and language!

Constitutional Law, jurisprudence, English comprehension, and critical thinking are still way beyond you. Now you know your ABCs, next time, won't you sing for me at that level? Amazing, the illiteracy. Get back to the store, and make sure no mistakes at the cash register and no dropping merchandise in the store, for they will cut, without mercy, from minimum wage pay.

No excuses and sincere apologies, which I offered to that foreigner, regardless, is an illegal taking away an American job! I was simply trying to see how calling blue-collar workers "deplorables" would sound, and it sounded horrid.

Learned Lewis, however, admired my humility in apologizing and said to me: If a Simple fellow like you, Snoopy, can apologize to an individual for a wrong, can we expect Joe to apologize to the Nation for Never-Ending wrongs, gaffes, and stumbles? My response was,

Learned Lewis, thank you! His apology will come in a concession speech in November 2024. He has much to apologize to America for!

That reminds me, would Broadway musicians, singers, dancers, etc., fall under that categorization of 'deplorable,' with that new "Stuffs" stuff being the true calling in life? To each his or her own, for with that, maybe she'll feel, She Coulda Danced All Night and Begged for More! One part of me thinks that the Feed the Birds (Tuppence A Bag) Lady Role would be perfect for HRC in a remake of that iconic Disney Film!

Learned Lewis: On an ominous note, the vicinity of St Paul's Cathedral should be cleaned of bird droppings, with the scare of Bird Flu - bird flu called H5N1. Personally, I am also scared of human droppings, aka human defecation, on the Banks of the Ohio and Muddy Mississippi, and other places, river banks, street corners, abandoned building takeovers, and much more than can be imagined. **Stop Ruining America!**

At the rate we are going with you willfully and blatantly encouraging illegal immigrants to stay in power permanently, Joe, you have no legitimate claim to remain in office. **Stop the Illegal and Unethical Persecution of Donald Trump!**

Venus: A Goddess on A Mountain, Shocking You Blue (Contd.)

Background from Learned Lewis:

The saga of Election interference is perhaps most strikingly evident in Georgia. The falsetto fence Trump's efforts to overturn his loss in the 2020 election were perhaps most prevailed in the race for the state's 16 electoral votes. But Trump and his allies spread lies about voter fraud, urged Georgia officials and state lawmakers to reverse Biden's win and plotted to send fake electors to Washington.

On Jan. 2, 2021, Trump called Georgia's secretary of state, Brad Raffensperger, and urged him to "find" 11,780 votes — the number needed to overcome Biden's victory. Fulton County District Attorney Fani Willis charged Trump and 18 of his allies for these efforts, alleging a wide-ranging criminal enterprise.

Fani Willis opened the criminal investigation in February 2021. She summoned many of Trump's top allies before a so-called special grand jury, which had the power to investigate crimes but not to approve criminal charges. In the summer of 2023, Willis presented her evidence to a regular grand jury, which approved a 98-page indictment on Aug. 14, 2023.

Simple Snoopy: Venus Willis is everything justice should not be – set-up, conniving, lying, cheating, and then with the audacity to act boisterously in court. I told **Adams-Apple,** a member of the Trump hate gang: Willis will imprison an innocent like you man for eating that apple eons ago. With regards to your misplaced allegiance to underperforming Joe, I said: **Why don't you search for someone younger with Swagger, rather than that Old McBide with a Stagger?**

Nostradamus Predictions

Few may know that the revered Nostradamus predicted in the 1500s that in 2024, the motives for the Georgia investigation into an American President would be laid out eons before by a Rock Group, called the Eagles, by their characterization of a Goddess Venus Like figure, now known as Wishy-Washy Venus Fani Willis.

The group, in fact, did on an album many years ago and poignantly asked then, actually foretelling what would be a dismal American chapter in American law in the future:

"Did you do it for love,

Did you do it for money,

Did you do it for spite,

Did you think you had to, honey?"

Whether Willis remains or recuses herself or checks out anytime, she can never leave the ignominious impression of the hatching of the plot and the scheming that transpired.

Since it was upstairs and downstairs in the condo and in the vicinity, as cell tower records indicated, someone called them Venus Willis and Wee-Willie-Wonka-Wade. Had Ella been around, been around, she'd say: Oh, Lady Be Good!

Learned Lewis: Wade Innocence or Guilt - Analysis from a Statistical Perspective

The Fani Willis' prosecution of Donald Trump may be alive, but it isn't well" after the ruling by Judge McAfee, and that famous "odor of mendacity" summarized the sordid connivance, which called for the resignation of Nathan Wade.

Just to recap, Nathan Wade (called Wee-Willie-Wonka-Wade by Simple Office Snoopy)- was a special prosecutor working with the Fulton County District Attorney's. He voluntarily resigned his post after the judge that District Attorney Fani Willis and her office could remain on the 2020 election case involving former President Donald Trump, with either, she or Wade retaining their place. Gentleman Nathan Wade stepped aside.

I decided to focus on exonerating or implicating Wade and decided to do some analysis using probability statistics, with the available data. Nothing is beyond our intelligence, and we were keen to put innocence or guilt to rest with this determination.

Likelihood and Cell Tower Data: Inferences Drawn

The "pings" bouncing off cell towers were the data that showed Wade to be in the vicinity of the condo during midnight to early morning hours, which only establishes the following:

1. Hippity hop, hop, of Wade near the condo of Willis, does not indicate definitive visits to the condo, mere agility.

   Inference: The possibility of visits to others in the area cannot be ruled out. Therefore, whether Wade is a Part-time, or Full-Time Lover cannot be concluded in the absence of more robust and precise data.

2. The nocturnal activity can only show the likelihood and probability (with 95% confidence) that Wade was waist-deep in something personal with anyone in that Zip Code, and whether he was zipped or not is conjecture, as that cannot be ascertained, for the number of residents is too many in that area to make any definitive assertions of engagement with one or more of any gender.

   Inference: Since there is no information/data, it is inappropriate to state or conclude with any degree of certainty or support, with statistical significance and conviction, that he was even there at his condo of Willis. Since there was no glove, you cannot see the fit, therefore, you must acquit! (paraphrasing Defense Attorney Johnnie Cochran). Our condolences and sympathies to the families of the late OJ Simpson – on both sides.

Stats: Wade has withdrawn and pulled himself out of the case; further analysis following his resignation, and this ends the analysis into this matter.

Simple Snoopy: Wow, LL, I am impressed but undaunted by your remarkable statistical prowess. I have what I believe is comparable, or arguably even more significant, connection as my inferences, as I see links to Joe Biden using his weaponized Department of Justice. From the looks of it, it is he who is a scheming racist, cleverly using the race card to manipulate black people as pawns. How do I say this? Elementary, My Dear Watson – trace the origins and source of things. It all points to the "Big Guy" in nefarious schemes galore!

I'll show you precisely how he is using race to give these wonderful but clueless people a bad rap:

1. All the important prosecutors are African-Americans – Bragg, Letticia, and Willis; leave the idiot Ergonomic aside, for he defies racial or any human sanity classification.

2. Willis made visits to the White House. She wasn't there to deliver pizzas or make powder supplies – cocaine was found there recently. It shows that Willis was receiving directions but got caught in a different way. Yank Ole and Smiley from the Case because Willis was visiting the White House to receive orders! Unless she is also in the Cocaine trade as a reason to visit the WH to make deliveries!

3. On April 2, 2024, it was reported that Brooklyn Federal Court Judge Nicholas Garaufis stated that members of the New York City Fire Department booing of Letitia James, pro-Trump chants was not about politics, 'has to do with race' is erroneous and fails to probe things at a deeper level.

4. This democratic voicing (boo's) of their feelings would not have happened, and our brave Fire Fighter not been vilified had state Attorney General Letitia James not campaigned in 2018 with racial overtones, which were from the divisive tutorship of party leadership – again all pointing to the racism – the very top using race to advance political positions, and by the same token, reaping other benefits, for which the 10% allegations and of influence peddling are being assessed.

It is really surprising, that this humble journalist is pointing this out, while it has not been the cynosure of more attention by the more intelligent than me. This divisive racial divide and rule strategy has led to cascades of racial segregationally offensive consequences.

Trump refers to AG Letitia James as having an "ugly mouth" and "low IQ" in a Truth Social rant, but it must be said, Lettuce has a far greater vile mouth, and her nasty comments about the Trump family predate a few years those comments in April 2024.

Besides, Trump has an 'NFU' strategy. Now I know, with the FU, you are thinking vulgarity. Actually, he maintains a Christ philosophy of offering the other check before unloading. It is called the "No First Use" (NFU) is a commitment to never use his arsenal of profanity first under any circumstances, whether as a preemptive attack or first strike, or in response to an attack of any kind.

If you look at the origins first, from where this all emanates in the Trump cases to energy, economics, and illegal immigration, these all point back to Joe, slow in all other respects but the fastest gun alive on the political vengeance trail – step aside Billy the "kiddo," Grandpop's is gonna teach ya the revenge dope-a-rope.

5. Young and old in America, In My (own) Way, "I'll state my case, of which I'm certain," citing the interview of presidential candidate for 2024, the distinguished Robert F. Kennedy Jr., with CNN. It was the real thing and no April Fool's Day stuff this April 1, 2024, when RFK Jr. chose Biden as the biggest threat to democracy because he felt the president had been "weaponizing the federal agencies" against his opponents. Concurring with the former President and millions of others in the country and all over the world, the Evil of the Empire.

Learned Lewis – further Information and Insight: For the world and the young in America, who may not know: An independent candidate for the upcoming Presidential elections in November 2024 is Robert F. Kennedy, Jr., known as RFK Jr. He is the nephew of America's 35th President, illustrious and famous President John F. Kennedy (JFK).

RFK Jr. is the son of JFK's brother, who served President Kennedy as his Attorney General - Robert F. Kennedy. Both were unfortunately assassinated: JFK in 1963 and RFK, Sr. in the midst of his 1968 Presidential campaign.

Important: Now forget Lee Harvey Oswald and Sirhan Bishara Sirhan – "Who killed the Kennedys, "It was you and me," – Jagger – Richards said and meant that it was the evil in the world. C'mon, Jagger, man, that's all changing. Now it's me doing all the killing (and it's not softly, for I'm no troubadour – just Big Trouble in a Very High Place) before they reach the White House.

"Let me, please, introduce myself.

I'm a man of wealth and (poor) taste

And I laid (weaponized) traps for troubadours."

(and for a businessman and an environmentalist)

A **Gary Clueman** replied to the discourse on "A Plot Twist in Trump's Georgia Case" with foul-mouthed babbling on a full moon day.

Response, thinking that this guy may be old actor Cooper, said to him. You are the chosen Asstronaut for the next NASA mission to the Daft-Side-of-Da-Moon! Rejoice, O Chosen One, as exploration to the Moon is back on the rails.

The ruling of Judge Scott McAfee on Friday, March 12, 2024, was specific, a veritable judicial imprimatur and subtle endorsement of the court, some say, in willful or skilled efforts, perhaps in Trump's favor. It was appropriately fine at casting doubts and questioning Willis' credibility in the public eye but did not go far enough, leaving wrangling for another day. Wade resigned a few hours later.

McAfee also suggested Willis needed to toe the line of ethical conduct in the future, as her conduct, although it did not merit disqualification, was "legally improper" and connoted "dangerous waters for the district attorney to wade into." The before and after this decision yielded many back-and-forth trading of 'barbs' in personal efforts to call for the system of justice to play out, rather than hateful rhetoric of those with little knowledge of the intricate details of the case and the workings of law and justice, and the recourse and rights to take things further by prosecutor and defendants.

But both the opinion and the extraordinary hearing that preceded it lend a hugely significant judicial imprimatur to Trump's successful effort to diminish Willis' credibility in the public eye.

Merryman: This gentleman from Sherwood Forest, Nottingham, UK, prowling the USA for retribution and to take back the country for his Majesty, King Charles, and take from the rich to give to the poor, on 16 March 2024: quoting McAfee after the disastrous and sordid testimony, said:

"Willis (whom I called Venus) may be punished appropriately elsewhere, such as the General Assembly, the Georgia State Ethics Commission, the State Bar of Georgia, the Fulton County Board of Commissioners, as well as the voters of Fulton County may offer feedback on any unanswered questions, but whatever way this plays out, the evil design of a weaponized playbook in conjunction with sowing the seeds of political aspirational grandeur in Willis saw the ebbing of the judicial system. McAfee was far from convincing and added to political drama rather than some closure and judicial authoritative firmness.

Simple Snoopy: Venus Willis was/is engaged in willful Election Interference! Fani Willis must recuse herself from the Trump Case and stubbornness could mean jail. That she has tarnished the image of law is an understatement!

As the Prosecutor, her own house (or condo) was not in order. The simple premise is - from Matthew 7:1-5 NKJV:

"Judge not, that you be not judged. For with what judgment you judge, you will be judged, and with the measure you use, it will be measured back to you. And why do you look at the speck..."

Drum Ron (Called him fondly the Elvis' Drummer, because I genuinely thought he was here with the Sweet Inspirations, but the foul rants indicated otherwise, and no Sugar-Sugar Sweets):

With due respect, the Bible does not govern the Rules of Criminal Procedure or the Rules of Professional Responsibility, although your irrelevant posting will save me a trip to Church this Sunday. With that said, if I were Trump, I would be VERY concerned if this trial is going to be conducted.

I seem to remember Election interference is what Trump did when he called the Secretary of State in Georgia in a rage, screaming to "stop the count" because he was losing... BIGLY! You are wrong, bro. Every vote must be counted, right? Except when Trump is losing...oh no, THOSE VOTES....

Simple Snoopy: The foundations of the law, which you do not seem to know, are derived from Judeo-Roman, English common law, and other sources. Go to Church and pray twice as hard for the health of those in decline. We do not want a default, President. Get educated on the origins and evolution of law, and end the infatuation with DT. Surely, you'd have other things in life, and studying rudimentary precepts of law should keep you busy.

Every Vote must be counted - had/has the right to make sure that was the case! "Seem to remember" is indicative of the onset of dementia and dim-entia. Look to the future, for Ole is going downhill BIGLY! - with the same as your ailment – lapse in memory, gait, but beefed-up evil trait - plural!

No exception. Casting a vote is a right, a privilege, and a responsibility. If there is any suspicion of votes not being counted or missed, the President has the power, immunity, and authority to ask for checking this out. This is a recognized fact in election systems of the world. Election irregularities occur around the world. The ignorance in this matter is remarkable. The Supreme Court has also advised all to tone down the rhetoric.

Also, look at policies and not individuals. Right now, illegal immigration is a huge concern. With the huge hordes coming in, we are inviting our beloved country to be like Dhaka, Mumbai, Shanghai, etc., with people hanging out of trains, buses, and similar to many countries, defecating on river banks and washing azzes (not misspelling – just to get past AI filters curbing freedom of speech) in the river.

If you see the open defecation mentioned in another place or even two in this book, it is because it is a serious threat and reality, and that is why it needs dinning in for voters – to ALERT and ALARM! Wake up to reality - look at the policies and make an informed choice. Your posts indicate only hate and the inability to look at what is good, just a one-track hatred for DT!

Drum Ron: In elections, there is one method to contest in a court of law, and the process is exhausted. Chump (and lawyers) tried that 60 times and ranted publicly about fraud. His lawyers, UNDER OATH, were also asked if they had found proof of fraud, and their response was always, "No fraud, your Honor."

Simple Snoopy: Oh, Chimp (suitable name-calling for Chump)! The process is not exhausted - understand the rudiments of law, the recourse, and the right to appeal Chimp! Spew the kind of Ignorance on the farm! This independent has the education to wrap yer around in circles of knowledge to set you on a one-way ticket to the Blues and the Moon! It would be one small step for man, one giant leap for idiot kind.

Replying to Simple Snoopy, "Ah, gotcha. You are just trolling. You got me! Haha...good one."

Simple Snoopy: Obviously, the tit-for-tat, Chimp for Chump, conveyed the point of "immunity" more effectively. Not trolling at all. In fact, educating on the nuances and intricacies of civilized jurisprudence, the recourse and right to appeal, the equal application of the law, due process, etc. and common sense - so uncommon all around.

Chapter 14:
Roxanne, Those Days are Over!

The readers must be introduced to "Roxanne." She is the central figure in the song by British rock band the Police, and written by the universally loved and highly talented lead singer and bassist Sting. Our interpretation only, which we found many using the same analogy, is that Roxanne now deserves to take a break from living the high and hard life, and so must Carroll.

Theories, all one-sided like the Trump Biographer as to why Trump Keeps Attacking Carroll in Wonderland.

Simple Snoopy: You hear too much of alarms and sirens. Clueless, quit listening to Floyds: The Lunatic is On the Grass, man. Although it's therapy for ya, it's worsening the brain damage and lunacy. Roxanne's dreams of grandeur are going to evaporate, as this is going to be thrown out on appeal!

Unknown: Hey Snoopy, you are terrific, and you must be related to the brilliant Snoop Dogg, are you?

Reply: By now, my name and acclaim as Simple Snoopy is spread to the far and wide corners of the earth. Forget the conceitedness, but readers of this book should know that Learned Lewis and I are very current musically as well. We both listen endlessly to the refreshing music as we see many, regardless of the lyrics, relate to problems that plague the disillusionment and disarray of the American Dream by Joe.

A few examples:

- Beyoncé: because of the stuff going on in Texas: TEXAS HOLD 'EM.

- Teddy Swims: Illegals swimming across the Rio Grande and fake asylum seekers: The Door – Gateway to the USA.

- Dua Lipa: Houdini, and how Donald Trump escapes the Sprung Traps of the Illegal Human Fur Trappers – the DOJ and the Axle of Evil, headed by Monster Slime in Grime and Crime!

- Artemas: The kiss of death of Judas Priest like traitors Bolton, Haley, Christie and other Slime, Dime a Dozen, Two-Faced Cans of Squirming Worms.

- Cardi B: Enough of Joe's disastrous policies: Enough (Miami).

Honorable mention of Adele, Swift, Clarkson, Cyrus, music from Kinderella, Barbie, and Jaws – yes, Jaws too, because that's the Big Evil Shark going after people whom they set their eyes and minds on!

Reply: Snoop Dogg is a brilliant guy as a rapper and actor. If imitation is the finest form of flattery, then I do that! Lip sync his stuff, try and act and move like him, and I do think I am getting better at it. No copying, though. He's just too good and inimitable!

Well, talents differ, and all is well and wisely put said the Squirrel to the Mountain, If I cannot carry Mountain on my back, neither can you crack a Nut – I'm sure Learned Lewis, Emerson is a part of the literary arsenal, but each day I am stealing a little of your thunder! Anyhow, he is fabulous at what he does and is super talented, but I think it's a draw because I'm no dummy, either.

Let's settle for that that we (Snoop's) are both Superior Among Equals! I must say, my focus is investigative journalism, and there are no copyright issues between the 'y' to my name. Snoopy is a key differentiator, with the brilliant Snoop Dogg, multi-talented artist and Grammy Award Winner. Now time to focus:

James Deanie said McAfee split the baby and rendered a cowardly decision. Requiring one attorney to resign, citing a conflict of interest, was warranted as prosecutorial misconduct existed, with sufficient evidence of lying to the court about when the relationship started.

The "cash payments", corroborating evidence and testimony, proved they both lied on the stand, which in and of itself is grounds for disqualification. This judge is trying to appease both sides. How anyone could watch her testimony and not conclude that she was lying is beyond me.

Along with the text messaging in the middle of the night and geo-tracking on the phone that placed him at her residence going back to 2019 proved they lied. Now, both sides will appeal, so the decision will only kick the can down the road and clog up the courts. Cowardly decision by McAfee, possibly the newness to the position and the inexperience – to cleverly play it stinkingly safe.

Tailored Cleo Liz: Willis purposely went after Trump to make a name for herself using an old, outdated law that hasn't been used in decades. She had a person she was bound and determined to find a crime. This case should never have gone to court in the first place, rather you are for Trump or not, the law is all the goal to have the law and then find the man – the latter is easy!

Rich Burton: Did he really lose control? He ain't that dumb. He programmed it and set it loose.

Learned Lewis: I must step in here to put things in proper perspective to quell the evil tirade and condemnation of a former US President by Tailored Cleo Liz and Rich Burton.

I believe that the Racketeering Influenced and Corrupt Organizations Act is a truly powerful law enforcement tool in the hands of saintly and unbiased prosecutors. However, when the prosecutors are motivated by illusions of conquering the world, of illusions of fame and fortune, and will connive to take down an important figure in the hope that this will overnight bring them global recognition, the law is immediately useless. Perhaps fine when used to bring to book corruption, white-collar crimes and the like.

The key word missing and cleverly downplayed is "peacefully" by Trump. A mob can go out of hand and turn riotous, but it was not orchestrated as an insurrection. Stop this baseless, party-dirty, putrid lies.

Simple Snoopy: The case of Willis and Wade is a smoking gun. He was in the thick of things, as a prosecutor, travel, getaways, divorce, etc., and firing on all cylinders! It is hogwash to suggest that payment for those vacations was from personal savings from his successful law business.

Jerry Mouse: I am not playing any games here, but the mouse has grabbed this kitty for a change. For Willis to continue on the case, more trouble lies ahead. The state legislature investigating, a new state panel is empowered to remove district attorneys, and the state bar and the state ethics commission could mean such malicious kitties will think twice.

Georgia Republican Gov. Brian Kemp on Wednesday signed legislation empowering the state Prosecuting Attorneys Qualifications Commission to remove prosecutors or impose other sanctions.

Simple Snoopy: Mouse, nice humor of Jerry going after Tom for a change! For 80 years, that cat has been, without success, trying to lay his paws on that mouse! You have this backward, though, in the way this can play out. Willis has been exposed already. This entire case gets thrown out. Justice cannot be served when grounded and founded on tainted intentions of personal aggrandizement in any shape and form!

I'm educating here (like Learned Lewis) as an educated subject matter expert (not an uneducated one). The success of Customer Relationship Management marketing programs, they say, is 50%. The interpretation of this politically is that there is optimism in Donald Trump winning, i.e. half success and the promise and optimism in convincing the other 50% that America has a better future with his re-election.

Both views are correct - the analogy applies here - there is weaponization without a doubt, regardless, open your mind to acquiring knowledge on unbiased justice, instead of a closed mind, one not allowing for the free exchange of knowledge. That is Socratic Thinking! Remember the wise Greek philosopher? Diametrically opposite views and polarizations and Americans pitting one against the other will lessen when both sides start beginning to see the light.

Carroll in Wonderland, Roxanne

Red Lights, on No More No More, Too Old Now to Hit the Dirt Road

Sparse and spacey, the ringy arpeggiated chords of Summers, the poetic Sting, and fancy beatin' of drummer Krupa Copeland, the Police and the character Roxanne in the song of the same name seems to be the perfect fit of has-beens Carroll in Wonderland, Roxanne, Flaunty-Jaunty Cagey Daniels.

The analogy is perfect. Carroll in Wonderland, perhaps, had a red light on to solicit and get men to the store to try out lingerie and use other such ploys, while the storms that the biblical character Flaunty-Jaunty Daniel faced in the Lion's Den are possibly akin to encounters with capsizing boats of men in the bad weather and blackmail.

The comparisons maybe pertinent to all this going by the continuous saga here of lying and deception and the finessed experience in the craft to taking this from the physical to the economics of artful extortion for big bucks. Now, it's open to the question as to why the judges presiding over such egregious miscarriages of justice are swayed by the illogical, a question we also asked in the Roxanne saga at the end of this chapter and could not get satisfactory answers.

Simple Snoopy: From these cases, we can extrapolate and also coin the word Prostitutorial Misconduct, relevant and applicable to Flaunty-Jaunty Stormy Daniels and Carroll-Roxanne.

Glenn John: "Prostitutorial misconduct! This new word with a whole lot of meaning! The only misconduct now in the definition of Prosecutorial Misconduct that applies to this situation is Prosecutorial Corruption, defined "as the misuse of public office and resources by individuals in positions of power at the local level for personal gain or the benefit of select groups."

By the way, now that the documentary from 'Britney vs Spears' filmmakers is out, the vocabulary, eloquence, and commercial instincts of Daniels come to the fore and five when she found betrayal in her celebrity lawyer Michael Avenati's dipping into the precious take and proceeds from her book: "You're in prison, bitch!"

Decaffeinated. This person with the name Decaffeinated was reminded that with the lack of understanding of the fundamentals of law and lacking of common sense, any monetary damages awarded by kangaroo courts and juries are not written in stone. When on weak foundations, these are invariably appealed and successfully overturned. So, man, understand the fundamentals of law to be taken seriously in the garbage you slyly throw into your neighbor's yard.

Nastiness personified **Decaffeinated**, passed nasty comments of language abilities, which Simple Snoopy did not take all that too kindly. Regarding the King's English, man-can teach that to ya, all the way from Milton's, and Shakespearesass, to contemporary lingo, profanity and vulgarity. However, I cannot teach the uneducated the fundamentals of law, jurisprudence, and the presumption of innocence - so quit delivering final Judgments before anyone else!

Also, as an unbiased analyst of the truth, Lingerie Carrol in Wonderland-Roxanne and Flaunty-Jaunty, Daniels-Stormy are practitioners of the oldest profession. The former needs to be caught by the Police, and we'll send 'em a Message in a Johnny Walka Bottle or some other brand of repute for the woman Lingerie Tryout Carroll!

Solar Panel: A clear supporter said: Carroll has done, and continues to do, what every GOP Senator or Congressman/woman cannot do, is stand up to him. Imagine an 80-year-old courageous woman to stand up to him and tell the truth. Trump is nothing. I hope this makes all of those like Tim Scott and so many others see who they are supporting...

Darryl: This guy expressed similar sentiments to the Solar Panel in a sing-song kind of way, which made one suspicious of his identify, so the response below.

Simple Snoopy: Ever since ya left Oats, you in the payroll of the Big Guy, eh, Hall?

Hate of Biblical Proportions

The sentiments are clubbed together for the reader from our research, as the commonality is with the one aim of disbelieving the other side, despite any proof or evidence contrary to specific to the claims of Carroll in Wonderland-Roxanne!

Slingshot David: Summarized here are the misconceptions and vile repetitious expressions of Slingshot and like-minded supporters of Carroll in Wonderland Roxanne. The problem stated by a few is that:

- Trump is gaming the system by appeals, delays, and attacks on others with intentions to drag the dirt and not pay.

- There is plenty of repeat of already appealed and now more lingering of his stench. **Misconceptions and Changing tunes with Correction:** He has FILED an appeal but will not necessarily be allowed to appeal unless he and his attorneys can demonstrate that an error was made in court and that effort contributed to his loss. Sure, as is the right of the appeals court to refuse to hear his appeal if his attorney cannot demonstrate error at the trial, which led to the $83.3 million decision against him.

- Trump must pay up, shut up and move on to his other trials, where he should be held accountable and sent to prison.

- The $65 million has nothing to do with her reputation, more on. It's punitive damages to make sure he doesn't do it again. It's probably not enough. Well, $5 million obviously didn't, so maybe $65 million will. Trump walked out after the $5 million and immediately defamed her again. It's been two days since the $83 million, and he hasn't mentioned her (except as a Democrat plant to interfere with the elections).

Simple Snoopy: High and mighty after slaying Goliath, such arrogance that you now want to deny the appeal and are no longer just King David, eh? One cannot be denied the right to appeal, which will reviewed to determine acceptance - the right is there!

You are mixed up on knowledge of rights - courts don't have a right, it's an obligation - such fundamental mistakes mean you are new to the legal system and law and basically ignorant, just wanting to show mighty smart, but the smarter will catch you – you can't fool all the people, all the time, just some, sometimes, maybe!

A review is an obligation - refusal and acceptance come later- Admit knowledge deficit, moron. Get an education here. No, Goliath is trying to bludgeon you with a club here! Biden is trying to buy the election, by forgiving loans of Jack, Jill, and many.

Slingshot David: Replying to Simple Snoopy - Did you actually descend into writing in tongues there?

Snoop: Whatever it takes to educate an idiot man - tongues, livers, gizzards, et al. You trying to show off with such nincompoopishness. Mess with someone at your level – at the bottom rungs of your educational strata, not at these higher levels, man, where one is needed to talk about Life, Liberty, Equality, and Justice.

Elizabethan Miss: Brutus to Cassius: "There is a tide in the affairs of men, which, taken at the flood, leads on to fortune..." I celebrate E. Jean Carroll's victory over this vile individual, who, time and again, has shown us his utter disdain, not only for women but anyone who has no utile value to him. Do try to keep up Page Snoopy.

Simple Snoopy: Really: "Braved the system and come forward" 30 years later- Shakespeare? Cleopatra or Desdemona? You supporting someone who takes men to try out lingerie, lies about the dress date of manufacture, doesn't remember the year, there's no record of the year, and then tries and impress with Elizabethan garbage?

Et tu moron? Will teach you Shakespeare's plays – the entire gamut of Comedies, Tragedies, and Histories, beyond Julius Kaiser. Far ahead of fakey's trying to quote Shakespeare, who regrettably supports, maybe a once young, promiscuous, and now this ancient, turned blackmailer, and a modern-day old lady of dubious intent, who is wound up and obeys commands for political mischief and gain – that's party loyalty and a puppet on a G string.

Simple Snoopy: So, you don't need proof? You don't need a date when this supposedly happened, not even an accurate year. You don't need witnesses. Here are 83 million instincts because we don't like the guy. Nice try, but all this doesn't work. Roxanne needs to try knitting and selling on the Home Network and keep her mind off evil plots. Otherwise is going to be in history like Guy Fawkes.

Perhaps you can counsel her on graceful retirement and the occupational hazards of remaining in this business at this age. For the folly of plots and plans, to focus on cooking pans at this age in life instead. Show her what befell plotters Brutus and Shakespeare's nicely woven tale of the Gunpowder plot in Macbeth.

To this false statement, education has been fully provided to you below. If you persist in spreading this kind of false information against the former President of the United States, a legal brain similar to my colleague Learned Lewis, very knowledgeable in the law, criminal justice and the democratic process, informs that there'll surely be someone to haul you in for defamation, and election meddling. However, you may hit paydirt with payments from Mr. Evil himself.

Burt Bach: If you think Trump paying for his crimes is election interference, you aren't an independent. Unless you see Trump worship as independence.

Simple Snoopy: Burt Bach, you are no Ode to Joy, and your groveling is a disgrace to the Bach Family of JS, Anna and others. Keep a well-tempered mindset and stick to songwriting, for outside of Hall and music, you are Zilch. It is pure ignorance that you'd call anything a crime, with what is a civil matter, furthermore something that is not concluded, in some instances *sub-judice*, under review, or in the appeals process. We'll get a muzzle and a gag order for your snotty snout! Get an education-it will teach you about civility, civil and criminal law, and the basic rights and obligations of private citizens and government officials under United States law.

Forensically Wise: Processing the Scene

Simple Snoopy: Hey, big bro Learned Lewis, to present here to every idiot whom I encountered telling me that Donald Trump if he has nothing to hide, should voluntarily provide his DNA will be impossible. This was how I tackled this absurdity, but I will defer to hear from your scientific and legal smarts.

Now, I am no forensic pathologist, or crime scene expert, but I rely on common sense, which I am finding sorely lacking. I told the nincompoops, that for DNA to be admissible, it had to be processed at the crime scene immediately (within 72 hours) and not suddenly thought of about 30 years late. More importantly, the automatic assumption of all those I spoke to was that Carroll in Wonderland-Roxanne had preserved somebody's semen (not using the three-letter word with a c here) on a dress, but she could not remember the year.

Oh, how I only wish the legal team had hired me. I told them that they needed to study and know the fundamentals of law first instead of this nothingness and being Zero Hero. My investigative and probing questions were using the language they know, not scientific jargon:

1. What DNA does she have? - do you know?

2. Do you know that DNA can come from different sources from a human?

3. Is it hair, stool/excrement, tissue, semen, vomit, or phlegm?

4. Tell me and if the cases were reported 30 years ago and was the crime scene processed?

5. Also, how are you sure she did not surreptitiously collect anything from the loo -one of those family washrooms in stores? (I must confess, I used words like shit, droppings, turd, rather than the above, and asked them if Roxanne could have smeared and pasted any of that on that dress, now that she is trying to smear him). However, with the greed for money, she wouldn't know that the quality of DNA from certain sources could be contaminated, have issues regarding integrity, stability over time, degradation, etc.

It is appalling that these motor mouths knew nothing of forensics and criminology and ignorance. I told them it is dangerous for America, with the elections close now.

Anyway, I now request you explain tastefully and better Learned One.

Learned Lewis: Aside from the nasty substitutes for scientific words, SS, I give you high marks. But don't get conceited, man, and be too big for your britches – **"We"** could have advised the legal team. Any DNA to be admissible and valued as evidence would require the following:

1. A human sample from blood, semen, skin cells, tissue, organs, muscle, brain cells, bone, teeth, hair, saliva, mucus, perspiration, fingernails, urine, feces, etc., are sourced from which DNA that can be obtained, extracted, or processed.

2. DNA evidence relevant to the crime should be collected promptly, i.e. within 72 hours, to avoid degradation and for scientific and legal reasons.

3. Different possibilities exist, is any incident occurred at all, which is not clear, as her memory has conveniently deserted her about the specific year, and any reference to DNA from her only shows that the ulterior motives were blackmail, unfortunately with no knowledge of criminal forensics. Just from a forensic standpoint, it is also considered necessary to obtain an elimination sample from everyone who had consensual intercourse with the victim within 72 hours of the alleged assault to account for all of the DNA found on the victim or at the crime scene.

   If it was group and consensual sex (was it?) in that unknown year, how do we exclude others, and who are they? If not, it is a dilemma like the Jeffrey Epstein case and the visitors to the island and on those flight logs. The most plausible explanation is her Carroll in Wonderland-Roxanne fiction and predation, seeing the perfect opportunity to try and blackmail a wealthy former President and current candidate.

My Inference: Pretty baseless stuff from Carroll in Wonderland-Roxanne that should have never gone so far and will be thrown out. **Predatory intent, my conclusion.** It's just Money, Money, Money: "In my dreams, I have a plan. If I got me a wealthy man, I wouldn't have to work at all. I'd fool around and have a ball."

The lines from ABBA, sung by those lovely ladies (and 2 gentlemen) with voices of gold and characters of virtue, show that greed is universal. It sure the heck confounded me, for I thought the Swedes could care less, or not at all, for money. Greed does not wane even at 80 because this plot was hatched in the 90s but instigated and evilly provoked over the last 10-15 years or thereabouts. Who's behind all this, I'd ask? No conspiracy theory here, but she and Flaunty are just not as smart as Monica and Linda.

Macho and Dainty Cinderellas, Try This Shoe to See How It Fits

We asked this simple question for and against the claims of Carroll in Wonderland, whom we called Roxanne, of a wide cross-section of the population in the United States and abroad, specific to the $83 million award. The question was as follows:

Ladies and Gentlemen: Please consider this question, and provide your answer: Let's say either you (husband, father or brother, for the ladies at home) or your son is accused by a lady of the night 30 years later, saying you raped her then, and she is unable to give you a date and year, as she cannot remember. Now, with not a shred of video surveillance, evidence, no proof, no witnesses, she demands an enormous sum of money from you. Would you pay her out?

We asked all to take up the gauntlet and provide an answer to the question. Now that we had the shoe on the other foot, it pinched, but there was a kind of hush all over the world. No response from the brash and the bold, and even from the recluses and hermits, the blue-collared carpenters, and ALL.

It was the sound of silence which made mobs think and is considered Good Vibration for justice and for the courts of appeal to see that blackmail is a given. However, there must be real ulterior motives to go after Donald Trump – Persecution and Election Prevention and Interference. **World, dispassionately look at this, and evil perpetrators of ugly games, hang your heads in shame.**

Some Responses by Simple Snoopy in the Saga of Extortion and Blackmail

Here are some of the Simple Snoopy and the Old One Roxanne, in regards to her claims and the ensuing conversations:

To Tom: You been singing now for years that She's a Lady, Sir T., but you've got it all wrong if about Carroll! She's Delilah and will give ya a Haircut, man, and that will be the end of your masculinity and drinking champagne out of a Shoe. Live at Caesar's Palace, Las Vegas.

Unlucky Toxin: Make him post a bond for the damages. Trump is going to try and hide every dollar he has. He will go into maximum delay mode. Now, what is going to happen when Trump keeps defaming her? Because he will.

Response: Man, you sure sound like your luck ran out Toxin! Looks like you were banking (bang for the buck) on the money coming in for Carroll in Wonderland-Roxanne. Were you the go-go between for her? Did you get a 10% cut?

Married Marcie: I hope the judge also issues a permanent injunction against further defamation. Monetary damages will not change Trump's behavior, but perhaps a few nights in jail for violating an injunction will. Let him pay $$$ for all the illegal deals in his life.

Response: What defamation? Did she wait outside stores in the Red Dress to accompany men to try out lingerie?

Sean: Bunch of Biden democrats on the jury. November will tell a different story. **Response:** Connery, you have this spot on!

Josh: He's just a whiny Trumpite Bitch.

Reply: Jeez-Josh, it looks like your mistress threw you out. Be a civil dumpster diver! Please tell us about your educational level, man. The world would wanna know how much you know about the rule of law, the judicial right and recourse to law, the tenets of equality under the law, due process, and those Greek terms.

C'mon, man, we'll be waiting for your response and will see levels of education, critical thinking, memory, remembrance, and recall to recalibrate you for dementia and senility or plain idiocy.

Doubting Thomas: Trump could have ended the case by giving his DNA. He has instead resisted that tooth and nail. He could have given his DNA, which could have saved himself $90 million but could also put him behind bars. Contemporaneous conversations corroborate her account. Trump was found liable in a court of law by a jury of his peers who heard the evidence and testimony. That's how criminal justice works in America. Don't you find it strange that an innocent man would fight a DNA test that would unequivocally exonerate him? If it were me, I'd do it immediately. Who wouldn't? I'll tell you who? The guilty party is. How can you defend a rapist?

Response: Doubting, we can see why Christ told you off! Since then, thy name is forever known for untruths and doubts.

DNA for Lewdinskys Dress pertinent then, different circumstances. That dress of Roxanne was in 92, 93, 94, 95 - she couldn't remember. Which woman, other than of easy virtue, would go in to try our lingerie for a man? If she did it for money, then that's prostitution, but for that lingerie-pawsy-groping stuff game, that's the same, or at best, a close second. There is no camera footage, no dates she could cite, and her memory has deserted her, like someone big we know.

Tooth and Nail, is a source of DNA, when collected during and at the scene of the crime! She charged a fee, possibly, and that's prostitution. Suddenly, 30 years later, she has an awakening prompted by the lure of money and directed by vested interests. Doubting Thomas, you are stupid, man, to say that after 30 years, he would have been put behind bars? I also provided him with the spiel on DNA collection, processing, and the whole 9 and 10 yards and shards of it.

Criminal forensic procedures and investigators at the time of a reported rape crime require the victim to get medically examined and processed immediately. Ideally, within 72 hours, during which time the specimen and evidence are then collected, which arms the investigators to go out seeking DNA, and which may even be collected surreptitiously from the perpetrator's coffee cup, trash, now matched to genealogy databases, etc. Watch Forensic Files. Anyone stupid to give DNA 30 years later, which may also have been planted, then and later, is simply ignorant. You lack common sense.

This is a civil case, so stop the rubbish, Thomas ignoramus sucky muck, telling us, "That's how criminal justice works in America." You have the audacity to speak such stupid and absurd ignorance despite me also telling you about processing a crime scene and DNA evidence.

Constance Clings to-Putrid Nonsense: Seen this guy, and he says the same thing everywhere. He's got hate DT stuff, all-ready ready for Copy and Paste on anything Trump - the Harvard mentality - he'll paste the same for every assignment, plagiarize himself and anyone with vicious abandon!

Your profound ignorance is hardly a shocker. It is truly appalling and shows a lack of any legal knowledge. Study for the law-entrance-LSAT and get a law degree. Even if you are denied, duke it out, for these Universities discriminate against students on the very grounds they pretend in their false mission statements. Look at the class action and other lawsuits against so many for deceptive practices.

Constance Clings to-Putrid Nonsense. Response: You have spewed plenty of nonsense, "Who rapes women in dressing rooms is having legal troubles." Do you know something the world doesn't? Put your name out there, man, if you believe what you are saying is true. Hiding behind online posts! Cow-a-ward-Edward. Copy-and-paste cheaters never prosper.

Constance La Plagiarizing Cheat- has been caught. The World - please be informed that this person pastes the same laundry list for every conversation on DT, whom he says DT "rapes women in dressing rooms." This ignoramus will be shut down, and the world will watch out for hate-stuff!! With the vigilance, he's not going to speak nonsense in a hurry, we hope!

Would Carroll Roxanne feature in the Guinness Book of Records with the highest award ever for the oldest professional of the oldest profession? Naw, it's gonna be thrown out! There is an unequal application of the Law, and his wealth and Presidential Status is a magnet to vilify and impose arbitrary fines, that are awarded on a case built on Icicles.

They (appeals) need to find out the demographic makeup of the Jury - check race, party affiliations, and donations to parties. This kind of nonsense should not be allowed to stand. These are unbiased expressions of many, seeing the vile, biased, and unequal application of the law, shattering the very foundations of equality upon which this nation was built and is being taken down.

No copy and paste, like the fake posts here. This is from a legal mind ready to take on anyone till the cows come home on the rule of law and jurisprudence and fearless in the pursuit of justice for the rights of big and small.

Simple Snoopy: Anything bizarre and ludicrous is and will be thrown out on appeal. Then, Caroll will need to go back to her regular job, age and weather permitting.

Montenegro: Thrown out on appeal based on what errors of law?

Response: Nothing there- was it in 92, or 93, maybe 94, or perhaps 95. Hey Hugo, your name-sounds mighty big and bad, but it showcases an ugly dearth of knowledge, bereft of justice and law, and the legal options to appeal horrendous legal decisions that are questionable in fairness. Such awfully piddly diddly awareness makes me ask how much of an education you have?

Here's verified information cited here from the public domain:

1. Carroll claimed it happened in 1994.

2. She wore the dress and had just met Donald on the street and tried on lingerie for him in the changing room.

3. Then put away the dress and never wore it again except for a magazine, which informed her it wasn't made in 1994, so she promptly and conveniently changed the year of its making to 95 or 96.

4. She claimed loss in income and death threats.

5. Deleted all the emails because she didn't want to hurt her lawyer, and somehow those recent emails cannot be recovered" (which famous people come to mind for deleting emails and using pseudonyms)? It's not very convincing and doesn't add up.

The appeal may be Trump's 'Gotcha' of you, Carroll, and you may yearn for the less stressful good ole-days, now that you are past the slime prime of your time. It's only hope with financial perversions to anxiously await a payday that will not likely come.

Montenegro: Replying to Simple Snoopy: I asked for errors of law in the context of this trial, the third trial. The issues you raise belong in the first trial. Even if findings of fact could be appealed, the appeal has to be attached to the correct trial, which is the first trial. What error of law about this third trial do you have?

Simple Snoopy: Response: I don't make any points to you-as you are not an authority on anything. An appeals process has the opportunity for the concerned officials to look at the case and can do so holistically, from different judicial perspectives *per se*- when, say, "you" asked for errors of law, it shows a terrible paucity - no knowledge really, just trying to impress. You are right only to the extent that an appeal in a civil case needs an error of law.

Errors - as in this case that are likely to be found are wide and broad, beyond the scope of a discussion here. Those errors will likely be many, and will be presented by the Trump legal team, and will require a thorough review of the case by the appellate side, etc., that is the issue. It is you trying to show deep knowledge when the demand "asked" is problematic.

The scope and breadth of this case are likely to be several and can include misinterpretation of legal precedent, ostensibly to show the faulty application of the law and much more. If depends on legal strategy how they approach this, and I am sure it will be laid to an unbiased review court compellingly, such that it is set aside, and pity the greedy, for all that seems golden, loses its glitter and luster when fraud, blackmail, deception are implicit!

Someone informed us in the discussions that Carroll cannot go back to her regular job as age and gravity have taken their toll! No slander since all information is from the public domain and freely available information! However, there's plenty of dirty lingerie and linen washed in public and fearlessness in freedom of speech.

Other Common Themes: Generally Abusive and One-Sided

- The vast majority of the damages were punitive. If Trump had kept his mouth shut after the first verdict, the judgment would have been much smaller.

- Proud of an American Jury, sending a message that continuing defamation matters and nobody is above that. Over ten times, the original judgment is a serious message.

- **Mike:** They didn't send a big enough message. The damages should have been in the billions.

    Response: Snoopy: How profoundly stupid. Do focus on rowing your boat to the other side instead of indulging in uninformed ripostes

- Donnie Still Won't Listen... What A LOSER...he gets his butt kicked by an 80-year-old woman. Weak and a loser all his life. Oh, seems like no mad tweets and comments after the verdict did not contain her name. Let him pay $$$ for all the illegal deals in his life.

- Mistakenly thinks that he is smarter than anyone else. Sooner rather than later, he's bound to learn to just keep histrap shut.

    Some are profiting with this mouth wagging and not stopping. Carroll said she was going to be donating most of the money.

- **Response from a Sensible, other than Snoopy:** Really! I don't care if you are a woman or a man. Now, anyone can bring a lawsuit against you for the same thing! No don't need any evidence. You don't need a time or date. You have to prove you didn't do it. Without a witness, to say you didn't do it, you're in big trouble! I don't care if you're a man or a woman. Stand by now. The floodgates have been opened for a new form of going after who you hate and for the money.

- One part of the trial is over, this is about further defaming her afterward.

- Even if you still think that internally, you lost the court case and must follow the law.

- Initially, it was 5 million, but then Motor Mouth had to pay the price, and now it is 80 million and could go up to 400 million. Wish I could buy E Jean Carol stock because it is

100% guaranteed. Trump will surely open his maw again and, probably within weeks, if not days, and pay dearly.

- **Simple Snoopy Response to a Pejorative Soul:** I will put you on a bridge over Niagara, that is built on shaky and flawed foundations and will watch to see your level of confidence and comfort. This analogy should give you a picture of the dread for Carroll and supporters on the contrived nature of the charges.

    Anyone informed, prudent, and knowing even a fraction of the desired goals of fairness of law and the inherent right to a fair trial and to appeal will know of the importance of judicial neutrality. Donald Trump will have the right to seek redress and invoke his rights to appeal for what should be clear, extreme unfairness and travesty, as the case and the decision have precisely what the law ought not to be!

Snooky's Hot Mike: Strangest Questions & Coincidences that Missed Ripley's

Here are some strange and bizarre possibilities worthy of Ripley's, and may fuel conspiracy theories.

1. **Quick on the Draw: Guns and Lies:** In April 2024, the news caption was: "Police took possession of E. Jean Carroll's unregistered gun after her testimony in Trump defamation trial."

    One **Wise Solomon said:** She (Carroll) could say she had legitimate ownership if she could prove that this gun was fighting and not for fun (from Leon Uris), unlike a man, who wouldn't be able to do the same! Carroll, now that Glen Ford is done with movies, you may now well be the Fastest Gun Alive – and you've got the groove and hook and do pull some fast ones, for which some fall hook, line and stinker.

    Do get that gun holstered, buckled to the chastity belt and registered. Per NY Penal Law § 265.00(15), for Firearms - Dangerous Weapons, a license is needed to possess a handgun.

2. **Remarkable Coincident and Cover-up:** Wouldn't it be some strange date with destiny and fate if the registration of Hunter's Gun and Caroll's were the same? Report that would be some coincidence if they were sharing the same gun someone on social media pointed out and covering up for each other – Both lie, so well that this would be within the realm of possibility – **Believe it or Not.**

3. **Lyin Eyes:** The CNN report stated that it would be the first time that the first time in US history theJustice Department has charged the child of a sitting president. OK, but is he a child? Hunter is not a child, so was he lying or CNN? The three charges include making false statements on federal firearms forms and possession of a firearm as a prohibited person.

4. **One God to Another:** Was that gun a family heirloom? Well, the history of music is replete with songs with hidden messages, different meanings when played backward and so forth. Just ask Bryan Adams, the Beatles, Lady Gaga, Bonnie Tyler, Bob Marley, Maroon, Pink Floyd and several others. But is there a hidden message from the God of Guitar, Jimi, to the God of America? You decide.

Hey Joe, where you goin' with that gun in your hand?

Both Gods are born in earthly incarnation just a week apart as pointed out in this book. Did Jimi foretell that the other God would be holding America ransom with policies (gun) that spell ruin and damnation?

5. **(Evil) God of America vs God of Good:** Different Treatments and Immunities for both Gods. A descendant from the House of Hur (remember Ben Hur – Heston) special counsel Robert Hur described President Joe Biden as an "elderly man with a poor memory" but did not recommend charges for potentially holding classified documents for fifty years in public office, and not counting, the reportedly earned advance income (a bird in hand, may be worth more than former President Bush) of 8 million bucks for writing memoirs sourced from materials in the garage, neighboring state university and other places for safekeeping.

The God of Good, on the other had, is charged by Beanstock Jack, the Giant Slayer, with the same for holding to documents for a year or two. You decide who is treated like God and who is treated like Shit! Then, the duo of "ugly" and "manic" mouths" with the former charging with compound interest, threatening for several years, and made good almost with the seizure of Towers and Treasures of millions in value.

Now, America and learned courts, this analysis itself will help you determine if there is a conspiracy favoring Bad God, who is using Evil powers against the God of Good.

Those were the top 5. Two others that did not quite make it:

- **Indictment and Conviction:** Most people in America do not know the difference between the two: An indictment is not a conviction. It does not matter whether it is handed up in federal or state court is a formal accusation. Put the reading glasses on, and this is a chance to increase from zero level of knowledge to 2, on a scale of 1 to 10! Don't forget what Bo Diddley said: "Before You Accuse Me (Take a Look at Yourself)."

- **Dora the Explorer:** Children's favorite Dora frequently says to the cunning little fox to prevent trying to steal from Boots and others: Swiper, no Swiping! Dora has added as an ounce of cure rather than prevention: Sniffer, no Sniffin!

Chapter 15:
There's a Kind of Hush: The Palpable Mush Honey Case

It is amazing that it is one man's name is mentioned as responsible for right or wrong, even if it is the machinery of an election campaign staff. A disgusting, personalized, vilified weaponization against one man by the name of Donald Trump! Prosecutor and Judge in the Hush Money Case say Trump fraudulently disguised payment installments as corporate legal expenses in violation of New York law. The so-called hush money payments are somehow to magically 'find the man to fit', and the larger-than-life Trump is the intended and hapless victim. Make him a convicted felon before the elections. Are you crazy to think that a large number of Americans, including constitutional law, legal experts and others, do not see this as a set-up?

When it is all said and over, expect a one-sided affair. Nothing is lost between renowned and respected analyst and TV commentator Megyn Kelly and former President Trump. Their spate was well known, although setting aside differences, predicted Trump would likely be convicted in the hush money case he faces in the accounting infraction in the payment to adult film star Stormy Daniels. It points to the ridiculousness of the jury system for a high-profile defendant where political affiliations for the opposing side make it impossible for a 'fair trial.' A legitimate transference of the case to another jurisdiction is an absolute must!

Kelly, with some despondency, noted that Manhattan went 92 percent, between 87 and 92 percent for Joe Biden: "That's where this is going to be tried. These are not Trump lovers."

Judicial Reform Imperatives: Of Loopholes and Lacunae

In this book, Learned Lewis and I Simple Snoopy, have cited many instances which call for judicial reform. The extreme weaponization and political cunning expose the lacunae in the judicial system, especially in grey areas, where there is no precedent, apparent and not-so-obvious gaps, or ambiguity in the law. The dispensation of justice and the law, with its interpretation, is normally intended for the people, not for diabolical machinations of holding on to power when sensing that the people's mandate may not be favorable.

In emerging areas of technology and related fields of cybersecurity, intellectual property rights, etc., it is quite understandable that technology outpaces the progress and evolution of law. The saga of the 91 or so weaponized indictments of former resident Donald Trump is alarming in either sheer lackadaisicalness of the law and reality, with the numerous conflicts and legislation bereft of clear guidelines, for instance, in presidential immunity for decisions in office, and after with respect to classified and declassified information for personal use, memoirs, and myriads of situations.

The quandary is both gaps, evil and the dubious interpretations of revenge, vilification, and revenge, and the manipulatively conniving of multiple actors, directed by one evil lead.

The recommendations here are that there are definitive solutions, which necessitate turning to multi-disciplinary approaches which govern human behavior, to close gaps and plug loopholes in the law. The disciplines of anthropology (man is a perpetually wanting animal), psychology, the social sciences, and management, to name a few. A GAP analysis from business analytics thus may offer clues on where there may be weaknesses in the law between the existing state and nirvana or the desired state.

Now, we do not hold at all that the judiciary is, or is not entirely at fault, as it does not develop and write legislation, and that the process, in a nutshell, is that through Congress, the lawmaking branch of the federal government, a bill becomes a law, with a different process in the House of Representatives and in the Senate. Nevertheless, the judiciary and others can offer insight by inclusion in the research process of a bill or proposal, suitable insight for transition to law or amendment.

The multidisciplinary research must include simulations and role-play between the Forces of Good vs. the Forces of Evil, as is the current political scenario – you decide Who's Who? Batman, and The Joker, the Clown Prince of Crime, the evil mastermind and one of the foremost supervillains of all time in any universe. He is Batman's .... Don't be swayed by age and frailty, for the revelations will also show who is the Baddest on the Planet – step aside, Mike Tyson, he'll do a dope-a-rope on you when he takes you behind the gym and beats the daylights out of ya, because he's evil, you are not!

Analysis of Learned Lewis:

Twisting New York Law to suit is the common ploy by making the business records charges, at best a misdemeanor, which is also past the statute of limitations, rise to the level of felonies, however, may not link to Federal law, one looks at a holistic interpretation, as I will explain below. Furthermore, while the legal team of the defendant would argue that this is a private matter, Snoopy and I think that Election Campaigners have the right to curb negative stories, ads, rumors, and anything that is against the aims of campaigning. This is a legitimate business expense. Companies allocate damage control funds for recalls, negative competitor maneuvering, or to dispel negative testimonials, word-of-mouth, and so forth.

The true aim of the prosecutors is to show the voters that they are voting for a criminal, nothing more and nothing less, which is election interference at the behest of the head of the rotational genius, the one who makes the world go around the Spindle, of the Axle of Evil! Rigged elections that happen for Putin, Saddam Hussain, and now Joe!

It is not remarkable much that the other side must try and bring women of questionable virtue, but scoundrels know all the politics. It is less about the unproven claim of Flaunty-Jaunty Daniels, perhaps a gnarled hand at ensnarement, in the art of the deal, but here, more in what has the markings of tutorship from upstairs – aka the Axle which makes multiple Wheels of Evil rotate, independently and in combination. Not smart enough to prevent Swiper Fox Attorney Avenati, but with the wisdom teeth, maybe indirectly to grind down the election of a President to a jarring standstill. Her signed denial of a sexual encounter/affair with Trump is now there in the public domain.

Regardless of this, in terms of anticipation of how this plays out eventually, and once it does, the ramifications in November 2024 will be a stark nothing. **It will only convict Joe of failing the USA.**

The DOJ, headed by the brilliant (perhaps his gloating and self-pompous appraisal before the mirror – singing Oh, Lord it's Hard to Humble) Garlick Bread and Ole Partnership) may have thought they had sprung the perfect trap (perfect crime really) for Donald Trump, but should he win, they will have proven to be the ideal marketing arm of his campaign.

Thought they had the Election interference, the world sees. It is the first of its kind by the oldest profession of blackmail, albeit with no evidence, as one side says, "It never happened."

Simple Snoopy: From the Listening Posts - with No Interruption!

Pardon the interruption, Learned Lewis. I would like to present the diverse side of discussions from just one recent discourse – far from congenial, anything on this wretched election is – on both sides. Appreciate the ignorance, humor and the presence of supernatural evil. It was with utmost restraint that I did not interject my tit-for-tat, as I paid attention to your advice that listening is twice as hard as mouthing, and that's why God gave us double the mouth number in ears. I am reporting some spewing of sewage in of different folk in their vile speech contortions here.

1. We Democrats are doing everything possible to rush the case through the courts to affect the coming election. You can call it election non-interference, but we'd put the best-endangered species poachers in the world to shame in how we can do this ha ha!

2. Each conviction or indictment is a badge of honor for Trump as it increases his poll numbers. The desperately contrived-to-fit makes the first-ever collusion and unholy alliance of Ole McDuck and his nemesis, the BeagleBoyz-to-Ducks, more scared than ever. A supporter or Joe grudgingly said: It's the reverse outcome actually. All the plunder is going asunder as Donald Trump is stealing from our blunder!

3. Hunter isn't in politics, but I agree, "peddling" or substituting the 'e' with an 'i' and it is pissing in the wind and writing in the sand of politics – there's nothing there. Grow up! Forget Hunter, coke and we don't need weed to do our reality checks! My grouse will forever be that we need someone younger and springier like Gavin.

4. Bragg is an honest dude carrying out orders, although Carroll is more fascinating to talk about. Wait a minute, if someone emerges from the Woodwork (or Gutter) and claims you (or your Husband) or your son raped her 30 years ago and cannot remember the year, you'd just Pay up, right? No video or any evidence, nothing, just the word of a Woman of the Night and Red Light, who Goes into Stores to Try out Lingerie with men, she meets on the

street. Those Who Would Pay Pay-up for themselves, your spouse, or your offspring, Please Raise Your Hands!

5. Reply to someone with the name **Guitarman Comes Alive:** The right to appeal is a fundamental one, especially when you are innocent. Confess to all the crimes, let the voters decide. He's guilty, there is no question of due process and fair trials. Nothing is going to be thrown out - from the cases of Hookas Daniels, and Carroll to prosecutions by Bragg, Willis, to Jack Smithereens. Now, as Zappa said 40 years ago, "Shut Up 'n Play Yer Guitar!"

Thanks, Snoopy. Now I will continue as Learned Lewis: Here are the Distorted Facts of the Case with the Truth:

a) Trump was buying Daniels' silence: **Lies**
   Truth: Daniels herself denied it happened in a written statement.

b) The payoff was to ward off a possible sex scandal in the final weeks of the 2016 presidential campaign: **Lies.**

   Truth is ridiculous, as election campaign funds are also to counter negativity.

c) Michael Cohen, Trump's personal attorney and "fixer" at the time, paid $130,000 to Daniels in October 2016, according to prosecutors: **Lies.**

   Truth: Vilification with innuendos and malicious terms of "personal attorney" and "fixer" aimed at character assassination to influence elections. Trump should have the right to counter sue in the eyes of voters, for personalized defamation and persecution of a candidate who has the support of millions of Americans and people across the world.

d) Trump reimbursed Cohen in a series of installment payments processed by Trump's company. Prosecutors say Trump fraudulently disguised those installments as corporate legal expenses in violation of New York law: **Lies.**

   Truth: Pure nonsense again. Prudent businesses seldom make 'lump sum' payments. Cohen lies to the living and will do so even in Hell, or Heaven if he lies to custodian at the gates, St. Peter, to get in there.

   Truth: These contrived charges have sought to disqualify the nominee for the Republication party in a series of charges, unloaded all at once to scare, harm, damage, and prevent his contesting the elections.

   Truth: America sees through the evil forces at play. The weaponization by the administration is on such a scale that it is impossible and outside the reach of ordinary mortals and is only possible by the direct hand of the Evil God of America.

The case, if any, was a misdemeanor in 2016, was never tried then rightly, and the statute of limitations has run out. Judge Marchant, please send your qualifications for assessment and family and your affiliations and donations to the party. Going forward, the onus is on the prosecutors to:

- Prove it happened first, with witnesses and evidence, and not on the assumption that it did. Refuting the allegation and damage control is a valid campaign use of funds, for if falsities are quelled, so the candidate profile is not falsely lowered in the estimation of voters. The characterization as "hush money" is a disingenuous dirty play by prosecutorial actors acting on behalf of the candidate from the other side!

- **Academic Vigilantes:** There is a job to do! It is a far stretch of the imagination that this is even a misdemeanor, and trying to say it is a felony should go back and see if Alvin Bragg and his team have plagiarized and may have suspect legal qualifications. Getting AI to re-assess the qualifications for their legal revenge is abhorrent and doesn't show the very foundations of the knowledge of law.

- Shed weaponized intentions, for the world is watching, and the American people will hold you accountable. Read further below why.

- Display knowledge and shed vile intentions that marketing oneself in an election, better known as campaigning, is a business where there are allocations of expenses to promotion, which would also mean counter bad press and negative publicity. Surely you know the different roles and responsibilities of staff, and what they are entrusted to do.

- The Biden election machinery and, likewise, the Trump organization are a large organization, and cannot physically know what every individual in the organization is doing in campaign activities.

Another Music Example to Convey Ridiculousness and the Undoing of Weaponization: This is as ridiculous as holding the CEO of United Airlines United Airlines for the mishandling of baggage checkers breaking the guitar of Musician David Carroll. He exacted his revenge using his rights of freedom of expression by releasing the song "United Breaks Guitars" to United Airlines' manhandling. His video went viral with 15 million views on YouTube, and the bad publicity cost United Airlines $180 million or 10% of their weekly stocks. Prosecutors trying to win the elections, therefore, let the ballot decide, not the orders from the Boss.

- Understand, the keyword keyword in the Federal Election Campaign Act is the **"wide discretion"** in the various budgetary allocations for small and large initiatives, within the Federal Election Campaign Act restrictions, of course, on the disbursements, allocations, and use of campaign funds. The definition of an expenditure, implies the ways to influence positively for the candidate and to counter the negative strategies of the competition. Understand the fundamentals of business, you morons.

Money spent on Customer Relationship Management (CRM) is to retain existing customers and to also win new customers. Why cannot the tainted and machinate justice system disregard these universal principles? Are you so scared of Trump that your evil minds conjure such foul acts to prevent him from progressing? Are you also engaging in blackmail in collusion with a porn star?

- Explain whether it happened or not is immaterial, but do explain:

  How is private prostitution a sex scandal when discreet, consensual and for a fee? – Although it was denied by the principal concerned herself. In which case, there it should not be called a hush money case at all. Instead, it should be called damage control to blackmail, ruining an election perpetrated by the opposition for the 2016 election, and again now in 2024.

  How can prosecutors aid and abet blackmail and moral turpitude?

The schemed interference means that the process commenced on April 15, 2024, has achieved its disruption to the rival's campaign schedule, in a series of obstacles to bog him down. A break in an unintended veritable forced hiatus of Trump from the campaign trail to precious time wasted at a first criminal trial in Manhattan for the alleged charges of falsifying business records in connection with a payoff to Stormy Daniels, a porn star who claimed she had a sexual encounter with him but denied that in a written declaration, stating it never happened.

In fact, there is a written and signed statement from her that it did not happen. The higher the climb, the lower the levels of depravity from the Axle of Evil.

Chapter 16:
Traitorous Turncoat Tendencies and National Security Risks

Our enemies like information on the inner workings of the administration, and they are always looking for chinks in the armor of the United States.

A Danger to Himself and the Country

John Bolton, former national security adviser, was in the Trump administration for a couple of years. In an interview (which had to be translated and filtered possibly for obscenities and other senile nonsense), he compared the dictator Julius Caesar, to Trump, saying: "He hasn't got the brains! He's a property developer, for God's sake!" Then concurring with Joe on the "assault on democracy" and threats to the country and an "apocalypse," is that Bolton is retarded to think that, as the ousted Trump's former national security adviser, thinks he'd curry favor with Biden for a post.

The only guy who liked that curry and Tandoori stuff was the all-spiced-up Bill years ago, and they had to clean up the spicy aroma of the White House then, which lingered years after he left the building. It made you think you were in the residence of an Indian Prince in a bygone era, possibly.

What's your esteemed opinion, Learned Lewis?

Well, Snoopy, let me tell you some truths as a literary, historical, legal, and musical buff:

1. It was a downright mistake to ask Bolton the Caesar question because Trump, for the traitorous conduct, has possibly asked in shocked dismay: *Et tu, Rusto-un-trusto Brute*? a Latin phrase, literally meaning "and you as well (you as well, you rusted, untrusted f-in Brute!?) The real words he used I have omitted and dignified, by not quoting the expletive, as it begins with the next alphabet.

2. Now, from a historical perspective, the last guy who had illusions of grandeur and who thought he was Julius was in the sixties, an old geezer named Ebenezer, as reported by a lass, as they say in Britain, i.e. a lady. She favored Pink, who is a very dignified person and doesn't play any games.

   Quite unlike Roxanne, the one who put on her red dress every time, she intuitively knew she'd be going to a hotel or somebody's secret abode on the night the right wad came along. He (Ebenezer) is possibly still there, in a home, on therapy, and unchallenged as the Emperor of Rome, but we'll have to ask "members of The Scaffold (and Sir Paul, whose younger brother was one of the informant composers) about that and provide an update on our website.

My friend, a former security person, is quite dismayed that this rusted, not-to-be-trusted, nuts-and-bolts former national security advisor is divulging stuff which only the inner circle of a President would know.

Quite treacherous and treasonous, and the real motive may be to see if Joe will ask him to hop on board. Now that his own agility has receded like his hairline, anyone with hopping, skipping, and plotting abilities is an immediate hire. With the nonsense he's peddling, it seems like he is selling something close to nationally confidential information, which is a violation of the trust placed in him by the country. There'd be no takers.

This friend thinks Bolton needs to be strapped, shaved, and sent to the institution which has Nurse Rachet as the head of its operations. The extrasensory perception is in the whiskers; without those, he's a not-so-meek, and weak Walrus, is his theory – I've never seen or heard of such a Walrus before. Nevertheless, we hope he doesn't meet Nicholson there, on the set of a Nest sequel, or with any real problems, as in that expected raucous bunch of rowdies, he'd definitely be the subdued one, but you'd never know, as cheap still waters run mighty deep.

Mapping the Psychological Profile of Leaders

Any information about the psychological profile of the President of the United States, which was privy to a national security advisor, can raise concerns, as can be used in the perceptual mapping of the profile of a United States President, current future, and also by and of others in the administration.

This mapping gives the enemy an insight into different probability decision-making propensities, pathways and scenarios (including influencing peddling, frequency of urination – aka piddling, and pedaling, i.e. exercise on bicycles to prevent falling and for fitness – called the 3 P's of Psychological Probability Profiling: Peddling, Piddling, and Pedaling – whew, quite the tongue twister) in the case on nuclear emergencies, threats, to blackmail, and other enticement situations that a leader may be inclined to act when confronted with in different situations in times of War and Peace.

Bolton has already violated his duty to the country in a traitorous fashion. You would certainly not expect current and past officials in similar capacities to behave in such a bizarre way. Regurgitating the same stuff has possibly now worn thin on the TV circuit as well.

President Barack Obama, in 2009, in Executive Order 13526, amended the previous and in place executive orders. The changes were specific to the classification, declassification, and handling of national security information generated by the U.S. government and its employees and contractors, as well as information received from other governments. The real aim is to protect sensitive and classified information, considered worthy of secrecy in the interest of national security interest and the potential damage and harm it can cause, in incalculable ways.

Let me explain perceptual mapping, a technique widely used in the study of marketing, consumer behavior and marketing research to understand the ever-changing and, at times, fickle minds of the consumer.

The technique can be applied to intelligence, and now, with Artificial Intelligence, it can be in more sophisticated forms to unravel and fathom the human mind. In this form of mind and perception mapping, strategists and intelligence experts often invoke studies and techniques that strive to model several critical aspects that govern human behavior, and turn freely to the disciplines of psychology, anthropology, the social sciences, statistics, and more to do so. They say the less intelligent and greater the greed, the easier mapping!

So here Bolton is on these TV shows all over the country. He could get invited to the BBC in the UK, then India, Russia, and China, and be like Jules Verne, spewing nonsense in 80 days and less. We wonder if the baboon was on one of those Chinese balloons floating around the United States and stealing secrets.

Not Going His Way

Important officials face the clear and ever-present danger of being kidnapped overseas. The Russians probably sent those captured to secret locations in Siberia. Have them bolted (no pun intended) or strapped down endlessly, with a drop of water falling on the captives' heads for hours on end. With a variety of other such techniques, the captive is ready to spill the beans and tell it all. God forbid, if ever such a situation may arise, all the highly classified and secret information will be divulged, putting at risk one to thousands of lives.

Bolton quit this nonsense, man; with this kind of conduct, you'll be rejected for even the security guard position at the local supermarket or greeter at Wal-Mart. But in the end, we all make our own choices. For Trump, given that security position, he may have regrets and say, "I've had a few, but then again, too few to mention," as Paul Anka or Frank often lamented, and God Bless their great souls.

One should know in politics that you are in an administration at the discretion of the leader at the helm. If, for any reason, there is a loss of confidence, blame yourself for not being in step and in tune with the administration's vision and policies, what's happening domestically and internationally. If shown the door, be careful it doesn't hurt ya in the rear. Well, maybe you have achieved remarkable things already and should thank your stars that you even surprised yourself and a host of others.

For Christ sake, for your own future, don't badmouth the boss, the President, or the administration, for you show yourself to be a bitter loser after getting your just desserts, as history is going to judge you as just that. Try and sell your memoirs, and any of that cheap stuff is quickly going to consign you to the dustbins of overflowing rubbish dumpsters over time.

Modern justice is no longer an automatic execution of traitors, so you are safe in that respect but don't undermine your own credibility and dishonor and forget who put you there in the first place.

Thanks for these pearls of wisdom, Learned Lewis, and true to my calling of being Simple Snoopy, an investigative journalist and one who also has the mission to get into the thick of things, to correct fallacies and mistruths perpetrated by John Bolton, Haley and Christie immediately are some who come to mind.

Bolton Mischievous Traitor Prompted Conversations

The urging to Vote for policy, not person. Make an informed decision - look at the Happiness Index! – served the purpose of making people think deeper. Polls are showing we were better off under Donald Trump. Ignore crank, creaky, and rusted Gone Bolton. Voters are going to discern what's best for the country, not unreliable and expired goods.

Chapter 17:
The Eclipse and the Comet in 2024

Some of the remarkable stories of celestial warfare against the Great Satan, United States, were Haley's Comet and the Sun and Moon playing more games to confuse the already befuddled American brains of the last four years, with the Eclipse in April 2024.

Brenda: This gal shows up and asks: Where's Twitlers healthcare plan from 2016 and what policies are you referring to?

Simple Snoopy: Lee, I will excuse you for being behind the times. Your last hit, Rockin Around the Christmas Tree, was in 1958, and in 2023 had a revival 67 years later. Thank technology and the relief Christmas brought last year for the woe and misery for many in America. We're glad you made it into the Hall of Fame, and it shows that anything good has lasting value and is true of good governance as well.

Brenda Lee, you remind me of Reagan, who had a few hits in Hollywood, and then was a super hit as the President of America! The current guy should be a One-Hit-Wonder, with an exit bunker strategy in 2024.

The policies of cheaper gas, home, and groceries, flooding the country will illegals, who are murdering and generally committing crimes and being released in a jiffy, are terrible. Check your polls and get recent. From recent figures, 76% of Americans feel they were better off 4 years ago. Let's hope you have a new hit and are not acting old as dirt like the Ole Guy! Your voice still delights America, Brenda Lee.

So here, as Simple Snoopy, I immersed myself in some gut-wretched conversations with this dude Barryman and others after doing some due diligence on John Bolton:

Barryman, King and the Like-minded Thomases and Pickles: on Trump 'Hasn't Got the Brains' To Rule as A Dictator, comment by Bolton.

Barryman: Nastily said to me, "Your Daddy didn't love you, or you just don't know who your daddy is? BTW - trump has no virtues."

Simple Snoopy in Reply: Manilow, all you can sing is Copacabana. Otherwise, for all his virtues, Trump is a somebody, while you are a nobody! Are you singing now on street corners?

You've got the talent, man! Rise up once again, gather yourself, and sing How Great Thou Art, and you'll be just that! Listen to how Carrie sings it and take a few tips on pitch, style, leather boots, and voice control.

Also, put on a Red Dress and some High Heel Sneakers too! Rewards out there for the vocal and other talents, man! You've got to burn the midnight oil, though, but too bad, you have to wait for that midnight hour, like Roxanne and Jaunty, to Pickett and Pocket your Pickens, till the hour arrives when no one else is around! Wilson told you that already.

Simple Snoopy, responding to Barryman: Actually, I know who my papa is. But they tell me that even from genealogy, they couldn't trace your ancestry. Someone told them it was Roger the Lodger, who needs to give a sample for the paternity test to claim ya! Too educated for you Gibb, or Manilow wannabes.

Barryman, you say vote for all Democrats. Vote for President Biden and Vice President Harris to keep our rights. Just Vote BLUE.

Snoopy Response: I'm saying, look closely, and Naw! One is too old, one just smiles, and she is the default maid-in-waiting - how about RFK? Has anyone looked at his policies carefully? Now, his genealogy goes back to before Marilyn, Jacqueline, PT 109, to some remarkable and illustrious forefather(s).

Regarding Vice President Harris, it's really funny, but presidential contender Vivek Ramaswamy said that it is ironic that Smilodon is associated with NASA and space probes. She wouldn't be able to spell AI, forget the large term artificial intelligence. That's her level of smarts as the VP of Mighty USA.

As a compliment, I'll give this to her, her smile would make Mona Lisa blush with envy if you placed their portraits side by side. Smilodon was the once-extinct saber-toothed cat, LL informs us. You'd rattle this sole surviving saber-toothed tiger at your own peril, as Joe realized at the last presidential debate. Ever since, he's her, yes, man, but it's really the ex. Harvard man running only the show, and not the money.

Bluesy King: Putin said recently he's supporting Joe! He likes the idea of giving away billions of arms to Afghanistan, as that removes all those armaments from the battlefield. If you have doubts, change your name to Thomas, and you'll be less in distress (pickle). What nonsense you talking, man - if he believes "in something more powerful than himself," he believes in God. Cut the dose of the hallucinogenic you are on, and enter rehab! I also told the gent **Santa on Scene**, who said, "The orange blob is going to jail."

Reply to Santa, Northern Lights: You are seeing double. The Shrink will mix some yellow to your red and you'll be orange. If it's lead paint, you'd sing joyfully like Leadbelly, with the girth on you, or perhaps, Garth Brooks.

RoadieToad: Strayed into a different stage, unfortunately, yet, Putin continues his misinformation campaign to get his well-groomed puppet, Trump, elected.

Simple Snoopy: Tried a different form of humiliation to tell him where he belongs, without sermonizing on law and justice thing, so said: Look, that's the reason you are a roadie for Van Halen and ACDC - lifting equipment, testing stuff, carrying instruments, but are kept off the stage during the show, because not star quality, just the average toadie roadie.

Practice your scales, and do some finger-tapping exercises and air drumming while the show is on, and you'll think in your mind – A Star is Born! Nothing wrong with that. We all want to Superstars! Few make it to the big league and stage but stay out of here, as you're uninformed about the cacophony of this high-decibel election stuff.

Study hard and practice big, and you could be the next Guitar Hero or God, and no concerts in Moscow! I'll tell you, if Trump were President, they (ISIS), with Soleimani and others taken care of, would think ten times and he'd also see they have no money to pull stunts like this off.

The pallets of cash to the Iranians and others mean an increase in terrorism drones for Israel's target practice, as the money is invested in terror! Hamas wouldn't have dared to brazenly abduct, murder, or sexually assault because they'd be bankrupt, and Saudi would prevent terror, as would be scared that Trump could take away royalties, spares, oil, and protection.

The Genuine Concerns of Learned Lewis: There is hope, and let's give peace a chance! Never again, this should happen to Israel. Get the Saudis and others in the region to be involved. Keep the mischievous Iranians out of the efforts at arriving at lasting peace and a solution, as they are supporters of Hezbollah, and their nuclear designs are a threat to not just Israel but to the entire region and, eventually, the world. The Iranians want to control Mecca and Medina, and their proxies operate in a variety of different ways, mainly to undermine Joe and the United States.

A nuclear-armed Iran will, in a heartbeat, go all out, with total disregard for human life, as their sole purpose in life now is in the destruction of Israel! Iran's supreme leader has opposed Saudi Arabia's control over two of Islam's holiest sites. Regional influence is critical and is sought by both Middle Eastern powers. This is a powder keg, as Iranian Ayatollah Ali Khamenei has emphatically said the holy sites of Mecca and Medina "belong to all Muslims."

There is more respect overseas for Trump, perceived as the strongman, compared to weakling Biden. His fumbles, stumbles, confused state, and apparent cognitive decline are watched all over the world, which has not helped.

Some just age biologically faster than others, and we feel sorry and sad, more from him overstaying his welcome, a fine and wonderful man, other than this Weaponization.

President Joe Biden mocked Donald Trump's financial struggles during a reception at a campaign event in Dallas on Wednesday.

"Just the other day, a defeated-looking man came up to me and said, 'Mr. President, I have crushing debt, and I'm completely wiped out,'" Biden said. "And I had to look at him and say, 'Donald, I'm sorry. I can't help you.'"

Trump in that week, filed a statement in court saying he was rejected by 30 companies as he sought help from to pay off his $464 million bond from his fraud case. New York Attorney General Letitia James was posturing to seize his assets if he was unable to pay by Monday's deadline.

President for the Good of America

In the end, President Trump, we don't want you to change. We love you, Just the Way You Are – Piano Man. We've borrowed that from you, but we hope you'll come on board to save America and to infuse a New York State of Mind that is good for business. I am sure it's a bad vibe and changed, and negative New York state of mind all over the world with the outrage of the vicious attempts of the ridiculous warped Ergonomic, faulty legal design and partner Lettuce James attempts at the ransom of half a billion dollars. Fortunately, it failed.

It seems that Taylor Swift may have been the Jean Dixon in her prediction in saying this about you, "I never want to change so much that people can't recognize me. Just be yourself. There is no one better. It's hard to fight when the fight isn't fair. Words can break someone into a million pieces, but they can also put them back together."

Your qualities of endearment are business negotiations, determination, and maintaining our position as the Land of the Free and the Brave! Keep it clean, Mr. President Joe, for as Americans, we love current and past presidents, and you are within that group unless you continue to do any worse than already.

You are currently not holding very well, the keys to democracy and tradition. Please keep it safe and we must all earn the trust of each other and of America! The weaponization perpetrated by cyanide-laced Garlic Bread is an affront to civilization. That sense of hate percolates every segment of the population, and that group gets larger every day, with rap artists, athletes, singers, the hard-working deplorable bargain shoppers, to all others.

Surely, Taylor cannot support this absence of the rule of law and harmless and innocent women being randomly punched in the face. Supporting this kind of side runs counter to what you say, "Not letting others define you," And as a role model, "Don't let others throw you off your game." Women should not have to carry mace and alarm chains in broad daylight – we love your songs and say, support who you want, but not bad policies and laws against Americans.

Fake Accusations of Slowing Things Down and Delays and the Constitution

The over-zealous propensities to find something dubious even in breathing is ridiculous in the responses on the other side of the fence, when Trump, through his lawyers, justifiably sought to delay the US Supreme Court obstruction for the criminal trial on charges of plotting to overturn his 2020 election loss, when they would rule in a separate case that would likely have favorable legal ramifications.

In a filing, the defendant's lawyers urged the Supreme Court to slow down the trial proceedings. This would be ideal for the justices to carefully weigh whether a defendant named Joseph Fischer, who was involved in the Jan. 6, 2021, U.S. Capitol attack, could be charged with obstructing an official proceeding. It holds significance, as Trump has been charged with obstructing an official proceeding and conspiring to do so when and although the word "peacefully" from him is deliberately hidden by the connivers. His exact words, "I know that everyone here will soon be marching over to the Capitol building to peacefully and patriotically make your voices heard."

Peacefully and patriotism are key, and in a democracy, "Voices heard" is crucial to be recognized. You cannot take away the right to free speech. Other than things going amiss, as in any frenzied riotous state, which is condemned and the involved charged.

Americans cannot be denied the right to free speech and assembly by those endangering democratic norms to steal elections!

Constitution of the United States: First Amendment.

> Congress shall make no law respecting an establishment of religion, or prohibiting the free exercise thereof, or abridging the freedom of speech, or of the press; or the right of the people peaceably to assemble, and to petition the Government for a redress of grievances.

Ole, You have Senior Support

Simple Snoopy had a discussion with a feisty old Granny!

OLDGramma: Yes, the excitement is so contagious that even Old Gramma jumped into the fray in social media, with a few nasty barbs against DT, and incurred a suitable response for the misstated and failure to understand that everyone is entitled to appeal. Take it, Gramma, that you are an old fartzey. You join the other two here akin to the 3 witches who met in Thunder, Lightning and Rain in McBeth! Seek your own level of ignorance because the awakenings here may not respect your age and senility!

As you go from here to Bingo, you'd get caught cheating at the card games, with an upset and angry mind, as you have been getting by undetected all these few years. Wish ya luck, and remember that your anger with DT makes other seniors smarter than you Gramma! You've been living in a shoe with the brood for much too long and need some fresh air! All in good humor - stay well!

Your vocalizations depict one-sided hate, manifested by challenging others to show "one" admirable quality. Being on the other side of the fence, unless you do not have the expressive powers to show what is not appreciable, that in itself is pure extreme. Try analyzing what is going on and indicate negatives of the other side as well, unless you think it's picture-perfect! Be magnanimous on both sides, if ever possible, and the world is going to be a better place!

Simple Snoopy: Looking at this with no rancor for either side, he (Trump) is leading in the polls, which is an indicator of the world seeing him as someone who enjoys the confidence of many, and shows his smartness is liked. An incumbent to the office can select smart people to serve. To be smarter than his haters or haters on the other is a big no-no! Appreciate rather than vilify.

Replying to William: How can you say what I am saying when I have not used your words? What I am saying, is surely some qualities make a large part of America like him. The problem may be that you are so consumed with hate and dislike that you cannot discern this.

In advanced research, there is a technique to set aside embedded beliefs in the subconscious and increase the gigabytes in the brain to be receptive to new ideas. Will have to do this on another day, however, as information overload can hasten shock therapy treatment, my man! We value the physical and mental well-being of you and our leaders.

Let's not set aside our rights. Liberals and All-Americans support Human Rights and have always aided the fight and protection against political and religious persecution. Live up to American ideals and increase your favorability and support base regardless of which party you belong to - for you are American first and do not believe in oppression, persecution, and inequality.

State of the Union Speech

The world evaluated what many called an amphetamine laced or "on steroids" State of the Union speech" written in super large script to see if Biden passed or failed in March 2024.

Simple Snoopy Analysis: Forget the eyes and the make, the sarcasm or the lack thereof. The safety of Americans first, the prices at the pump, and the standard of living - all in precipitous decline! We do not need wheelchair wizards of nothing. Lives lost in Afghanistan and Billions of Dollars in equipment - that itself is enough stupidity to go around forever! Then add to those disasters Hamas terrorism in Israel and the festival of kites by Iran later in mid-April 2024.

C'mon Joe, is the hard trembling to be firm in domestic and foreign policy? Being a good man is fine at home, not to lead the most powerful country in the world and hasten almost singled-handed its decline.

Every American should visit large African and Asian cities to see people hanging out of buses, trains and the squalor - Make America Safe! America, not Ole Rhetoric! Expressed views on Biden's State of the Union Speech in a civil and analytical way, but the intimidation and cyberbullying are terrible.

Not interested in supporting or countering the thoughts on democracy when the dangerous disingenuousness of the weaponization runs counter to the very principles of democracy - where the tenets espoused under the jurisprudential principles guaranteed in a democracy are violated - notably of equality under the law, the presumption of innocence, due process, the freedom and rights of free speech, to appeal and recourse to equal justice, the safety and freedom of Americans, and the right to equal opportunity are taken away.

You are merely for a limited term in office and on earth and have no right to alter America! The efforts to change the demographic landscape by the illegal flooding of the country with illegal immigrants, to remain in power till perpetuity, is already showing what you have done with the chants of Death to America in America in Michigan, Frisco, New York and other places in April 2024.

Don't try an impose through intimidation, for it will not work. Hardworking Americans will not allow freedom of speech to be taken away with intimidation and will not piggyback on the comments of others for moral support.

Learned Lewis and Simple Snoopy: Response to Vibrant: Vibrant said the female vote is declining, and so is the black vote. He was trying desperately to jump on that Midnight Train to Georgia, and that seemed like it had left the station, based on what Glady's told us.

Reply: C'man, ole man can barely walk up flight stairs, you think he jumps on trains?

The female vote is going to go for DT - to show they do not support Red Light Roxanne. Ask the Doobiesabout jumping on trains. Those trains have no place for laggards: Down around the corner, a half a mile from here, you see them long trains runnin' and you watch them disappear.

Michelle: Not this election. Women will decide who is president. Michelle on "E. Jean Carroll lawyer claims Trump once called her a coded version of the C-word after a deposition."

Biologist Blue Jay, received an earful for being unaware of the vastness of law. This is not Biology, where everything is classified into vertebrates, invertebrates, and cut and dried. The right to a fair trial and to appeal means the legal options (depending on the case, these could be *sub-judice,* in review, to be determined legally, etc.- all too confusing for clueless Biologic moron) are never shut down with finality.

The defense has the ability to exercise different options to determine illegality, bias, and so forth - the nuances of the law will be beyond, with no grounding to understand the presumption of innocence and equality under the law. As a biologist, we commend you for saving the planet and protecting wild and other forms of life. Any expert opinions on the law would require study, for legal knowledge, as of now, is paltry – not poultry.

As a favor, please listen to Stevie-Wonder's Mistra-Know-It-All. You'll understand the stark-nothingness your arguments and spews hold. You are just asking questions and seeking answers congruent with the dimwit personal-one-shaded-spectrum, which happens to be an intelligent forum. No one will let you get away with persistently imposing ignorance on the gullible. Furthermore, the wrong phrase "point-out" because 4 fingers of mighty ignorance are pointing back at you in all you say!

Casting Aspersions

You have contradicted yourself. Muller and his report wasted millions of $'s, and he has faded away ignominiously. The focus is on the future and not the past. There should not be weaponization of justice for vicious and partisan politics, for that taints the noble profession of law. Again, I repeat, let the law of the land from the highest levels play its part and demonstrate wisdom and the acuity entrusted upon them in the finest democratic traditions.

Open Defecation an Illegal Migration

Defecation on the Banks of the Ohio, Mississippi, or other rivers awaits with illegal immigration, plus people hanging out of trees, buses, and trains, like in Mumbai, Dhaka, etc. Defeat the Ole Dimwit disaster!

Young dimwit, I'm joyously educating, and you have been receiving free education, and multiple lifetimes and reincarnations would be needed to come anywhere close to knowledge and education here. A short and long sentence is needed to educate ya!

Chapter 18:
Grapes are Sour, Jilted Losers

The top among the exalted list is former Representative Liz Cheney, whose disgruntlement and jealousy know no bounds, and even goes to the extent of a warning to the United States Supreme Court on the presidential claims of former President Donald Trump's immunity. The deliberate role in the House committee investigating the Jan. 6 attack on the U.S. Capitol seems fabrication is in the genetics and down to the bone. Remember the Weapons of Mass Destruction fabrication from the curled lips of Dad in the Bush days, Cheney?

Admit it, few have the charm, poise and grace of Obama, the suave of Bill, and the straightforward business sagaciousness and bargaining skills of Trump. Not presidential material, fence-sitting Romney the snake always, in some surreptitious ways, will always align with the other side of Trump.

Equal Application of Justice and Law: In December 2023, Romney said that he did not see 'any evidence' to authorize Joe Biden's impeachment inquiry. Which is fine, for let the presumption of innocence be the equal right and preserve of all.

Snoopy response to a Defender of Biden: Let the investigation take place to determine impeachment – that was done for Trump! If they have the votes, it will be so. If you are concerned, say your prayers, and if not concerned, ask for your prayers to make America safe and prosperous - so either way, you win, as you are praying for the good of the country, not the frailties of human nature - and we will all be blessed in abundance.

Romney just cannot get over Trump, elected once and strong in 2024. He's been jilted since he's the Man Who Thought He'd Be King – aka President - therefore, he'll see which way the wind blows and try and hitch a ride. Maybe with ego, aspiration, and disappointment, he never saw the good side of the Trump city. Oh, if only Tina was around, we'd ask her to sing this to the new reverberations, as only she could, and of course, Mr. Fogerty would rasp it as well for us equally well, on the Bayou, or anywhere, outside of Utah!

Simple Snoopy: Jealous and smitten Romney wants to stay relevant. He should not retire, just shut up and go away! A jilted man with a venomous streak! Good Golly Snoopy! Sounds like Biden you are describing. He's the jilted lover, to be as destructive as possible, yet with a fake facade of righteousness!

Team up with Romney, Liz, and Christie, look for a deserted Island and be their President and VP for life, or the disrupter you are, convince the Mr. Hyde side of you and Utah to cede from the Union! **Boots Randy** also disagreed that Romney or any Democrat would be 'an upgrade' over Trump in 2024" and were vociferous: What a pathetic loser. If he was a Democrat, he'd be ruining it as well. Grapes are sour. One look from this guy and milk curdles! Wow! That sums it up quite nicely for Mitt Romney.

Giving Romney Some Credit

If anything, Romney got right to Biden's own words and asked to join him in retirement: 'Time to transition." Ostensibly, he was concerned about all the noise of "Big Guy" and 10%, with the propensity to dispensing money with such largesse. If there is a violation of the FCPA, etc., that runs counter to the responsibilities of high office and conduct which be expected in it, even if the individual is bereft of a conscience and thinks she/he will get away with it, sooner or later, it's gonna get you and double the freaky stumbles and fumbles.

In the end, this book doesn't detract from the fact that all Americans, regardless of political ideology, persuasion, gender, ethnicity, national origin, and race, are truly magnanimous and wonderful. Romney absolutely is in that wonderful category, and despite his falling out with Donald Trump and avowed critic, he accurately predicts he will win reelection because of greater maturity.

The support from "young people and the minorities," the groups that were swayed with "gifts" by the Obama administration, gave to key voter blocs, including African Americans, Hispanics and young women, as Igor Bobic wrote in the HuffPost. He can see the support of Americans and the distress the country is going through, and it's time to mend fences and join with the winning team to make his own prediction come true.

Chapter 19:
Conclusions and Delusions

The legal stuff aside, this is really a Tawdry Tale of political machinations, mendaciousness and skullduggery with the "Get" handcuff and shackle Trump evident! All Americans from all walks of life decry the injustice!

An avid partisan hack was quick to point out, "This criminal's trials have deliberately been delayed endlessly, and it is evident that we live in a two-tiered justice system, one for Trump baby and the other for everyone else. Any citizen with 91 felony counts against him would have been in jail by now.

Name any other private citizen in US history to get as many as 2 Supreme Court hearings in a lifetime. Trump has asked for 2 this year--and it's only February.

Reply by a Prominent Native American: The ghosts of my native ancestors will tell you partisan hack that you speak with a forked tongue. Big Chief has made this country all his partisan hack. He's got the bow and arrows, the other side has just the bow. So, it's a heap of rubbish that favors the other Chief, who is put on the reservation, and they are threatening to even take that away.

Snoopy: Well, Partisan Pooch, you are part of the mob that doesn't know the darndest thing about the foundations of what the law is premised on. That is the presupposition of innocence first. Just imagine the vilification and the "Get and Convict" Trump" as the world watches the unprecedented weaponization - that is why Rap artists, African Americans, Hispanics and Americans are seeing the elongated prosecutorial vengeance.

As an analyst, the view is that the tide is shifting for DT as these groups have seen Trump represent hope for their future and aspirations, and they can also relate to the persecution. Ole needs to be replaced, for he has done little to nothing for 50 years in public office. The loss of words is embarrassing, and the increasing favorability sentiments that started as scattered flurries are now an avalanche of support gaining momentum with each day.

If intellectual property rights make it possible for creativity, ideas, inventions, and innovations to be recorded, registered, patented, and protected. Since there is formal and legal protection of intellectual property rights, there is another argument or question: Why should idiocy, an art form that some are endowed with, be not also afforded some form of legal protection, some may rightly ask? Every day, an idiot is born, and some last a lifetime – of course - all in jest and wishful thinking.

Even Comics are Serious Now!

There is extreme disillusionment in the ranks. Even veterans and stalwarts are piping a different tune to save face and sound the alarm bells at the rise in Trump's popularity with each indictment, and set aside in some form, James Carville for one. Master cynic Bill Maher, who has lived in

HBO and other homes, said: 'He'll do everything he can to make sure' Trump isn't president again, and fears he'll take Guantanamo Bay, or whatever comes.

Someone suggested to Maher that this is possible, and here is how to do it. Become a hermit, go into seclusion like Kaczyinski, and you would never know who is President. Just don't try any white powder tricks and mail-in-rebate stuff! Staying relevant - is his goal to earn his next paycheck. Earn the dime with some slime has always been his thing, reason and rhyme.

Rabid Huskydawg, an ardent aficionado of Maher, was outraged and howled, demanding an answer to why Maher could not be right. Simple Snoopy vehemently replied: Don't have to back opinions for a husky dawg. Since when did you believe that such an entitlement and a response is owed.

Even if they (social media) muzzled you and rejected ya, here, this one somehow escaped their attention. The reciprocation to an insult, you will see, is expected for a foul mouth.

Be pleasant in the world, for huskies are not supposed to be rottweilers, and you'd not have any mates in the pack - speaking of friends. Regarding Maher, he was thrown off HBO for a while for nastiness learned from you, which is ample proof of his offensiveness tendencies, but when they joke on him, they say he's the frowniest and most displeased jerk on the planet!

Please, those who live in glass penthouses.... forget they do or have done and use slingshots and cheap shots. They, however, get caught when their own dirt is dug up.

Jon Stewart, a comic after his return from a black sabbatical recluse, tried to make an untidy stink about Trump and his properties. Stewart was taught, look in the mirror – you're not so funny! He had overvalued his home by a whopping 829% in NYC.

Complacency or amnesia, after all, he could be biologically far older than his 60+ years and thought his overvalue' of his NYC home would go unnoticed, as he disputed the absence of victims and fraud on Trump's $454 million appeal bond.

Revered newsman Geraldo Rivera and journalist, attorney, author, and political commentator Rivera zeroed in on Rachel Mad Doe, whose nearly 30-minute on-air objection to the original hiring grabbed headlines. Clearly, a more balanced set of whiskers compared to a ton of bolts and substance none.

Game Changer for America: Evil vs Good

The election in 2024 is surely going to be the most earth-shattering and shaping of our lives, at least for America.

Anticipating and managing the complexities of impending and possibly wayward change of the future requires us to make wise ballot choices, favoring policy that is good for those that live here, not immediate healthcare driver's licenses, and commit a crime and not a blind eye off the hook you immediately go, for more! Good policies and electing who can offer to use safety, better health, lower prices and a better standard of living, should be the most important considerations to evaluate – not a carefree *Que Será, Será* (Whatever Will Be, Will Be).

The 1950s, when written by Livingston and Evans and sung by Doris Day in the Hitchcock film The Man Who Knew Too Much (1956), was ok for then, and perhaps even later when Sly (Sly the GOAT) and guitar virtuoso Feliciano sang them. Now we have The Man Who Knows Not Much, and the nightmares caused by Krueger and Hitchcock are like a Midsummer Night's Dream in comparison to what Americans can face and should not continue into the next 4 years and even ten years after.

It is we who must take these matters and choices into our own hands and vote prudently and look at the different forces acting in concert, and in isolation to have set-ups to prevent the other side. We are resolute and adaptive by nature because the USA gives us so many blessings, which politicians undo.

Our ingenuity and innovativeness will be vital in staying ahead of the curve in managing turmoil and change that has already arrived but requires vigilance in understanding evil and set-ups. Critical thinking, communication, education, and being informed, and, of course, strategies to thwart the setups we see at the ballot computers.

Juan Manuel Marchan, in the Hush Puppy case, as of April 2024, is more the merchant of vengeance and negative influence in buying, even bullying the jurors, evicting those he sees as doubtful to where he wants this to go! He's kind of like Henry Ford – you can take any turn on the road as long as it is left.

It's plain and simple; the Hack is premeditated, monkeying around with this monstrosity of a set-up against the grain of unbiased justice! Informed and prudent to cast aside the evil shadows of gloom.

Chapter 20:
Musings IV: From the Desks of Learned Lewis and Simple Snoopy

The weaponized brought on board with great fanfare Jack Smith, who has gone about his task with extraordinary all work and no play doggedness, that even bringing a bitch in season would not have diminished his one-track mind. Anything built on political vendetta is fraught with the discovery of underhand and disguised contemptible intentions, so it is no wonder that the learned Supreme Court has quite well curbed the legally reckless impetuousness of Jack Smith with a not-so-fast buddy.

Their ruling as of April 2024, when we are reporting, is a significant setback for the special counsel, who has taken every opportunity to try and bully all into rushing things. This is a bulldog bully, who is unleashed to create terror and a panic frenzy, but in a truly democratic setting, it will not work, despite the pressures of the Axle of Evil, from where Election, not Law, is the aim, i.e. interference, win at all costs, never mind the bollocks, we've got the pistol in our hands, and the DOJ is in our pockets. Can democracy not be threatened with the commands of an aging politician, on the wane and exit, to threaten and subvert the legal system?

Quote from Snoopy: He's an Irishman in DC who has lost his sting, but carries a mighty bite!

All the delays do little to appease the hate of the many, as anything favorable to Trump is promptly chastised in the most abominable verbal abuses hurled and denunciations possible, as called using any excuse and angle to delay the cases. The incitement should not deter the genuine pursuit of ensuring equal rights and justice for all. The Supreme Court is the guardian and custodian of rights and civilized democracy.

In this book, we have frequently called for patience, and not haste in tracking down the origins of weaponization. The Supreme Court owes it to the 70 to 80 million Americans to make sure that their probing and reviews do not ever forget that. This Jack may be quick, nimble, but he's fulla .. for his impulsiveness and haste to intimidate the Supreme Court, in what is intimidation, bullying, for quick and expeditious action, which is itself contemptuous.

Even after this is all said and done, to look closely, not at his argument, that a president's "constitutional duty" in respect of the law does not "entail a general right to violate them." But where the law is unclear on immunity, the more serious violation of the Constitution is ongoing and unprecedented. The current weaponization is with impunity, the immunity is taken for granted – don't you see it? The world does!

Genuine Citizen Concerns of at least Seventy to Eighty Million Americans

In all fairness to Smith, his persistence is like a dog chasing his tail. He'll go round and round, never giving up, but his work ethic and industriousness are not a problem. It is the tunnel vision, which is, by the danger of blotting out everything, much to the chagrin of critical thinkers, scholars, and others. The relentless pursuit, with the support of the administration, adds up to a totally weaponized system intended to stifle opposition, cripple their ability to contest and devalue completely the voters who are not aligned with their party.

Just out of curiosity, many would like to know if he – Jack Smith did the following:

1. Study the assignment given to him, the time given to do so, or is he learning on the job in prosecuting the cases, which would be a great disservice to the country.

2. Receive, secondly, in the orientation, were there any instructions from the man above the man, either directly or indirectly?

3. Prepare, thirdly, merely prosecuting war crimes in the Kosovo War is a different ball game from looking into Constitutional matters, as the people in the United States would like to know his background and suitability of this level of work, for the nature of it he has the right background to analyze, where there is no precedent, where the law is murky, non-existent, and still evolving.

4. Fear, as everyday citizens, our intelligence to ask these hard questions, which must not be questioned, and later targeted and harassed. Going by the clear weaponization, bringing obscure laws into play to harass and intimidate means that these are KGB and Gestapo techniques being applied for the first time in a democracy. By the way, the very definition of democracy is falling by the wayside, not just in the United States but also abroad. That will be another project in time – perhaps the Downward Slide of Democracy – Departures for the Time-Honored Traditions of it. Is the DOJ willing to be open to an internal study to probe and measure this decline, if any, to the degree and extent that it is the current position and where it is headed? I am sure the Founding Fathers will be pleased to receive and review such a study and report.

5. Lastly, no one can deny that all Roads lead to Rome and Caesar! Psychologists and profilers do not believe that the profile of Attorney General Merrick Garland has the wherewithal, sagaciousness, and independence to put together a slew of weaponized charges to the level and degree unheard of in civilization and the history of our republic. Somebody has overplayed their hand, and America knows it.

The Supreme Court has the patience, the wisdom, and the calm to look and probe deeper, for then and therein would likely lie the real story as to how the unheard 91 indictments were plotted. It is a deeper probe warranted to get to the real monster behind this and determine what the cover-ups and distortions are. Time and patience are there to uncover, for such travesties should never be allowed to threaten our democracy again for the next 100 years and more.

Learned Lewis: The 5th Amendment and Psychiatric and Psychological Testing

From a legal perspective, very specific to the Fifth Amendment are the rights of a jury trial when charged with a crime, protections against double jeopardy and self-incrimination, the right to a fair trial, and protection against seizure of property by the government without just compensation.

Most elements of the Fifth Amendment and the actions of whom Snoopy calls Judge Ergonomic and Prosecutor Wilting Lettuce seem to blatantly rather than precariously infringe these elements of the Fifth Amendment, which we leave to the courts to reject on appeal.

Our premise is that in view of their persecutory monstrosities against Donald Trump, the point one finger, four are pointing back and "Judge not, that ye be not judged" philosophies warrant their evaluation from a psychological standpoint for Lettuce and psychiatric treatment for Ergonomic, a design gone wrong.

Expert psychologists can assess, for example, the possible underlying reasons for such extreme racial hatred for a white male, in James' background, if she experienced racism, the need to get even, the reparation and similar issues, and wanting to be the first female Robin Hood. Why not? If Kamala Harris has strong emotions and deep resentment of the bussing in California, those scars, which run so deep that she brought those up against Joe in the last election debate. Ever since she's the real giggly deal and he's the acting lead dog, while BO commandeers everything with the 'work-from-home' behind-the-scene strategy, in compassion in part for age, but mainly as a cover-up for not seeing the lack of brains as the side-kick of eight years.

And what better opportunity to get, even under the guise of law, to do this to a former President. She (Lettuce) swore she would have her day in public appearances and speeches, at least known from 2018 onwards. The courts need to look at reverse discrimination very closely, as the exuberance in the declarations in any manifesto, whether Nazi, DEI, etc., can lead to zealots who get carried away – forget the female Robin Hood, she seems a Female Hitler, Snoopy says.

With party hatred, coupled with incitement and clever manipulation from the Axle of Evil, it's a fatal concoction of hatred! Fortunately, brilliant layers, critical thinkers and everyday people as fast catching on to the deviousness of the Axle of Evil, and it were not for the remarkable Bravery of One Man, the world would likely never know, and he would easily be castigated and thrust into the Hall of Shame, banished to ignominy and disgrace, with mud all over his face – but that's not going to happen.

The People of America are not going to be led astray by evil design – rest assured America and the world.

No Suspicion and Suspicious Minds: Fact Check for Reality!

The total of false and draconian charges framed in isolation and concert against one man, a former President of the United States, is well beyond imagination and points in no uncertain terms as merely with the specific intention of being so crippling, that it would be impossible for him to ever emerge in an economic, physical, and mental state, to even live, which seems to be the aim. Contesting elections aside, the aim is to hurt and devastate to such a level that it needs to be probed by a neutral international body.

The common citizen will be forever fearful by this precedent, for if the DOJ, ostensibly subservient to the administration, has gone about against one man with such intensity, it stands to reason that every citizen, and minority included, should be mortally afraid of terror unleashed if the administration is spoken against in democratic traditions and with free speech. The evil by the Axle of Evil and its radiating tentacles needs to end!

The confidence and trust of the people need to be re-earned, and only a neutral body can conduct an impartial and thorough investigation into the actions of the DOJ vis-à-vis Donald Trump. Learned Lewis (a minority himself, will leap out from this book and make this happen for America) can put together such an independent body, constituted from around the world. We cannot go around the world preaching democracy when our own house is a blatant portrayal of the violations and abuse of Human Rights. The CVs of officials such as Garland are impressive, but are they steeped enough outside of the prosecutorial nest to the wider connotations of human rights, which they may be unwittingly or deliberate and machinated violation?

Immediately, many Americans are very superstitious about the 50 years of political life, now that the writings are on the walls and halls of injustice. All credit to Stevie Wonder and Jeff Beck for the inspiration of that thought and to Elvis for the Suspicious Minds and Suspicion themes. Many now will ask whether it has been good luck for one and otherwise for the other side. Crookedness in the DNA, or acquired over time, more so, maybe a combination of both on the ladder to the top and the vilely evil machinations to stay there – the true purpose of the aging veteran at the game, now in attempted dwindling swindle of America.

Common wisdom from our knocks and spooks in life is that you can fool some people, some of the time, but when you try and do this to all the people, all the time, the fear and superstition give way to wanting to look closer. The scarer then becomes the 'scared', and the defense mechanism creates machinations, like spokes from the Axle, going outward, empowering from the core to the rim, all who can "get" the man! Suddenly, well-oiled operations that use camouflage and mendaciousness (thanks to Judge McAfee, the word is like a little salt in a dish – you cannot do without it now) forget that most in America are Smarter and can see through the pawns, sinister ministers, and nefarious designs.

Digitally Remastered from the 1700s for Home Truths in 2024!

Borrowing from one Irishman, Oliver Goldsmith, from the 1700s, on the hypocrisy of another in the 2000s (the last 50 years actually), is 'An Elegy on the Death of a Mad Dog'. I am sure this book will boost the sales of this digitally remastered hit single from the 1700's, as its lines, fit Lucifer's Anointed One to a "T"! Please do read!

Those in the Axle of Evil, other than "The Boss," included are the upper echelons of power, to the lower-level implementers, or as he said, in the elegy, "mongrel, puppy, whelp and hound, and curs of low degree, are all in this evil saga and charade!"

Many in the country from all walks of life and also persuasions would like to know more about whether these are miracles and divine intervention, or where lies the pointing of fingers, that point back, and at whom?

Coalitions, Communications, and Brotherly Lowe

The progressive flavors worldwide today are for partnerships, empowerment, innovation, teamwork, and all or everything that spells and means collaboration and cohesion. Yet we will also see the acts of desperation by leaders with poor strategic and management capabilities invoke and rely on control and invariably flounder in a changing global environment. Innovation is incentivized to happen when people are encouraged to see things differently, and we are lucky to have the internet to learn of good law, its abuse in application, and even downright meanness. In the end, the astute survive, and we (all Americans) want to be better at going forward.

Biden and Trump are urged to build coalitions of no Evil and great Good, respectively, from all spheres of American life, regardless of who gets elected. Make or live up to the promise to Keep America Safe and prosperous. Let's not be the financiers but have an equitable share in international peace-keeping, negotiate fair trade, and correct the protectionism of countries that exploit us and have ours as an open market but cleverly shield theirs. Increase the safety and well-being of those within while keeping illegals out! Increase the opportunities for Americans First. With our prosperity, we will be more generous to communities around the world and keep them where they are. Those who want to come here must do so legally.

The protesters on San Francisco's Golden Gate Bridge, to the 50 people arrested after protests disrupted traffic in Loop, near O'Hare Airport, Kennedy Expressway and elsewhere on April 15, are not traffic but human snarls. One can lay a wager that there will be a significant number of fake asylum seekers and illegals in those mobs. Wouldn't that be the real insurrection, then? For their seditious acts are to upend the American Way of Life – Thanks, Joe, for your policies. Own up and take the blame, man!

Chapter 21:
Crookedness and Desperation for Power in Perpetuity

Learned Lewis theorized to me, Simple Snoopy, why President Joe Biden has favored the massive illegal immigration and did nothing to stop it for almost three years, erroneously believing it would be a walk in the park (or a basement strategy) continued to run for a second term for him. After all, he had the machinery all set up for the wiles!

I am saying humbly, Joe, as you contemplate more mischief against Donald Trump:

Don't, Don't, Don't

Don't Do it! We are Watching!

Let's hear out **Learned Lewis** on his reasons. I value his wisdom and seeing what others miss inadvertently, deliberately, or perhaps a combination of both:

1. **Aim:** Create Power in Perpetuity for the Democratic Party. Get the illegals in and put them on a path to citizenship. Driver's licenses, educational and healthcare benefits, legal help, and a fast track to citizenship. This strategy and would mean forever loyal and indebted migrants in millions, who will, in time, show their appreciation and affection at the ballot for their saviors and benefactors. Change the demographic landscape forever. In short, the party's aim! The same aim is mirrored elsewhere in the world, i.e. in Pakistan, India, etc.

2. **Reality Check and Correction:** The miscalculation of Joe, was that after the legitimate 2020 victory, he assumed an unassailable advantage over President Trump. The aim was to mortally wound his opponent, with a string of lawsuits, using the strongest possible terms, with charges brought about by his Department of Justice, such that it would be impossible to ever recover and recoup. A miscalculation indeed, for the bravery of Donald Trump, the name of this book, the brilliance of his lawyers, and the ever-increasing army of supporters, who see injustice.

   The exponentially increasing support is for the injustice that no human being should ever be put through, and every official concerned should be (or will be) remorseful and hang their heads in shame! From the discriminated against minorities, white-and blue-collar workers, academics, intellectuals, professionals, the common man, the everyday Joe, without the last name Biden, are supporters of the awakenings.

3. **Protection of Legacy:** Last, but perhaps not the least, and maybe the most important part of this postulation is, is that if the party remains in power for many years into the distant future, the other 10% Big Guy stuff (if there and true) gets camouflaged and hidden forever. But they say the best-laid plans of men and shady mice usually go awry and fall apart. It is the reason, that change is warranted in the important agencies of the government, from the top, to down.

Americans want to hear the truth! No vendettas and vicious witch hunts, later, but transparent investigations by a very neutral body comprised of distinguished legal minds steeped in the principles of jurisprudence, the equal and unbiased application of the law, the presumption of innocence, and the principles of liberty, equality and justice, so wonderfully enshrined in the Constitution by our visionary Founding Fathers, who envisioned, "This land is your land, and this land is my land, From California to the New York island, From the Redwood Forest to the Gulf Stream waters. This land was made for you and me" - with sheer simplicity and gratitude by Woody Guthrie!

This election is going to be the most significant ever! Learn what is happening, see what you are experiencing, and make informed voting choices. Remove the lens of party narrow-mindedness, purge the heart, body, and soul of hate, if any, and set aside the blinders meant to prevent horses and dogs and even beasts of burden from getting distracted and spooked. The most important decisions ever are to be made in November 2024.

The quest for building a thriving America First must be to facilitate innovation with an empowered culture and environment and transformational leadership. Open your minds, for it is for future generations and America! We are too good and talented as Americans to suffer. We can begin anew by making the hope, success, prosperity, and safety of tomorrow – a reality and ours.

Quick Guide of Top 10 Characters in the Book: Antonomasia in Parenthesis

Humorous and Truthful by Snoopy and Lewis of Unethical Tyranny & Villainy

1. **Arthur F. Engoron (Ergonomic Faulty Design):** is an American judge serving on the Manhattan Supreme Court since 2013. He presided over the New York civil investigation of the Trump Organization in 2024. A five-judge panel of the New York Supreme Court, Appellate Division, issued a ruling on Trump's appeal on March 25, 2024, against the deadline for posting a bond to appeal the ruling further. The court reduced the bond from $454 million to $175 million, extending the bond deadline by ten days. The court also stayed the portion of Ergonomic Faulty Design's ruling that barred Trump from acting as an officer or director of any company in New York for three years pending appeals. Still, it allowed the installation of an independent monitor to proceed per the initial ruling. Trump posted the $175 million bond on April 1, 2024, which Lettuce questioned, but was shut up.

2. **Attorney General Merrick B. Garland (Garlicky Bread):** Sworn in as the 86th Attorney General of the United States on March 11, 2021. Holding responsibility as the nation's chief law enforcement officer, his weaponization makes him an omnipotent and all-powerful Attorney General heading the US Department of Justice (DOJ) with a strength of 115,000 employees in the US and internationally. Typically, the leader of the Department of Justice is dedicated to upholding the rule of law, keeping our country safe, and protecting the civil rights of all Americans, however, the reality from the analysis in the book indicates the very opposite in following the orders and instructions of a higher authority, called the senile God of America.

3. **Attorney General Letitia Ann James, New York (Withering/Wilting Lettuce):** Letitia James campaigned in 2018 with racial overtones and open expressions of the motives of vendetta to go after Donald Trump and the organization. The campaign promises were so disgustingly obvious to a fair-minded society, seeing how those who swear to uphold the truth are themselves evil and guilty of deeply embedded unfairness.

The 67th Attorney General of New York won the 2018 election as a member of the Democratic Party. James is the first African American and first woman to be elected New York Attorney General, which is commendable. What is not at all laudable, however, is that once called to serve in the hallowed halls of justice, swearing in public to use the position for political aims and aspirations is a travesty and a mockery of the finest and noble aims of the judiciary and justice. America is shocked and a disbarment should be a consideration, and the setting of an unlikely precedence is truly desirable after the nation has witnessed such vile persecution. Tainted judicial officials should not be allowed to politically interfere in bringing down political opponents when directed by political clout from the top, something that the SCOTUS has alluded to recently.

4. **District Attorney Alvin L. Bragg, Jr. (Alvin and the Chipmunks):** The 37th District Attorney elected in Manhattan, from Harlem, has served as state and federal prosecutor. He is the first Black DA in the history of the Manhattan office, which is fine, but justice transcends racial favoritism. It must be made starkly clear that all 34 counts of the charges of this same charge occurred outside the five-year statute of limitation, defy common sense logic, the rule of law, and a hijacking of the law. The pathetic grounding of Bragg's charges is the warped contention that Trump's "tolled time" outside New York City allows prosecutors to go beyond

that period, even though Trump's whereabouts as a larger-than-life figure were never a secret. Initially, he did not see the case with merit, but then hero Coca Colangelo arrived on the scene (see below), and where there was nothing, there were suddenly charges famed. One can see the inducement and motivation of Coca-Colangelo as politically inspired and directed by the Supremo Uno.

5. **District Attorney Fani Willis, Fulton County, Georgia (Venus Willis):** DA Fani Willis charged Trump and 18 of his allies by alleging wide-ranging criminal acts and omissions of the enterprise. Fani Willis opened the criminal investigation in February 2021. Before the connivance and improprieties of cavorting and colluding with hired prosecutors Nathan Wade surfaced, she had summoned many of Trump's top allies before a so-called special grand jury, holding power to investigate crimes but not to approve criminal charges. In the summer of 2023, Willis presented her evidence to a regular grand jury, which approved a 98-page indictment on August 14, 2023. Thereafter, her nefarious sexual and financial escapades have brought a lull to the judicial activities, as detailed in the book.

6. **Elizabeth Jean Carroll (Roxanne, Carroll in Wonderland):** An economic predator and possibly a practitioner of the oldest profession, aside from a day job as an American journalist, author, and advice columnist, accused Donald Trump of sexually assaulting her in the mid-1990s. The brainwave to do so was 30 years later, with no recollection of the precise year, which initially cited, was found incorrect from the year of manufacture of the dress. Carroll sued former President Donald Trump in the United States District Court for the Southern District of New York (originally filed in the New York Supreme Court) for defamation and battery. New York is a predominantly Democrat state, which is now possibly changing, as may be seen in the massive turnout for a Trump rally in May 2024.

Trump denied the allegations. On May 9, 2023, a jury found Trump liable for defamation and sexual abuse against Carroll and awarded her $5 million in damages. On January 26, 2024, a jury (despite the lack of evidence on her say so) found Trump liable for defaming Carroll. After his remarks after the first verdict, the insane judge awarded her an additional $83.3 million in damages. Trump appealed the ridiculously astronomical verdict and posted a $91.6 million bond.

She (Roxanne-Carroll in Wonderland) has the predatory and opportunistic instincts to wait for 30 years to stake a claim and the world sees the impossibility of this being anything but politically driven connivance from the highest levels. A New York politically biased set-up will indict anyone with the name Donald Trump. A generally held view, and in common parlance, tainted juries and judges will disregard the truth and absence of facts and will indict even a luckless **'ham sandwich'** – and that is never farther than the truth with the cases here, machinated to tarnish his name and image and hurt his success in the elections in November 2024. Judicial reform is but inevitable with such a sad state of unprecedented political vengeance. All these unfortunately politically driven cases by a weaponized justice system against the former president will be overturned on appeal, is the view of unbiased political and legal experts and common folk in the United States and those who are watching the drama of human deceit worldwide.

7. **Judge Juan Manuel Merchan (Merchant of Vengeance – of New York, not Venice):** Presiding judge over the 2024 criminal trial of former US president Donald Trump. He holds many unusual firsts 1) as a committed Democrat with a donation on record and his family also making donations and likely profiting from the publicity the case brings, therefore in clear violation of the ethical tenets of expected judicial neutrality. The biased conduct was watched by the world and was widely regarded as a disgrace to justice 2) the first judge in history to preside over the criminal indictment of a sitting or former US President, and 3) the first judge to hold a President in criminal contempt of court.

A Democratic Party loyalist who abdicated his fair, unbiased, and neutral judicial responsibilities (instead of recusing himself) decided to somehow interfere in the electability of former President Donald Trump in 2024. In so doing seems to forget there is a higher authority in Lady Justice watching. The man upstairs who frowns upon such conduct and will hold him accountable on Judgement Day, but hopefully also sooner – tainted to this degree and for this most important case is regrettable.

The New York judicial apparatus needs a radical change of working overhauls, spectacles, and dressing up to purge the weaponization of the system and ridding of systemic political and racial bias, of the kind found nowhere in an advanced civilized democratic system, with populations less than that of the United States.

8. **Matthew Colangelo (Coca Colangelo):** A former senior Biden Justice Department official, is a lead attorney in the political prosecution of President Trump with Manhattan DA Alvin Bragg. While his persuasions are for now secret like the formula for Coca-Cola, it is well known that this prosecutor of Trump instigated Bragg to take up the prosecution against Donald Trump. Quitting a top DOJ post for a far smaller NY job smacks of doing so with inducement with promises of higher aspirations and positions to **'get at all costs'** former president, similar to the distinctly dubious efforts of Jack Smith, Fani Willis, et al.

Human ambition and greed for higher positions, with the right levels of incitement and lure of reward will make liars and cheats out of humans – Cohen thought he would be a top official in the Trump administration and got caught with lies. Perhaps investigations will reveal how educated humans like Coca-Colangelo can be so delusionally radical, forget their responsibility to society, their legal training, due process, and judicial fairness as seeing the chance of bringing down a former President as a once in several lifetimes gift from God!

9. **Special Prosecutor Nathan Wade (Upstairs and Downstairs, Wee-Willie-Wonka-Wade):** Was a special prosecutor working with the Georgia Fulton County District Attorney's Office, with no experience in the assigned responsibility. A sexual relationship with DA Fani Willis, financial improprieties, and romantic getaways surfaced, connoting connivance and collusion. He was left with little choice but to voluntarily resign his post after the judge on the case

McAfee ruled that the "financial cloud of impropriety and potential untruthfulness" as seen, meant that the District Attorney Fani Willis and her office could remain on the 2020 election case involving former President Donald Trump, with either/or, she, or Wade remaining on the case. Just imagine the scheming that would have continued had they not got caught, all in the name of justice.

10. **Stormy Daniels (Flaunty-Jaunty Daniels):** Daniels, 45, whose real name is Stephanie Clifford, is an adult porn film actress. Yes, a star whose fortunes could shine bright temporarily but will possibly be thrown out by the jury in an acquittal in late May 2024 or later on reversal. A woman of easy virtue used to set up the case by zealous, politically galvanized prosecutors and a tainted judge, even after she provided in writing that the affair did not happen. Their attempts to bootstrap a simple clerical error, with anything felonious only depict the desperation and morbid fear of the impending victory of Donald Trump.

Ms. Daniels provided salacious details of their alleged sexual encounter in court while Mr. Trump sat in the same courtroom several feet away. She, after a written statement that did not happen, now claims that she and Mr. Trump had sex and that she accepted $130,000 from his former lawyer, Michael Cohen, before the 2016 election in exchange for her silence about the encounter. Call her a call girl, hooker, hustler, slut, lady of the night, or whatever. Still, it's the greatest and most sinister use of this professional Flaunty-Jaunty Daniels by a political foe, by the Axle of Evil, from where all the evil radiates. Attempting to win the elections using prostitution and hookers is truly deplorable. C'mon man, do better than that!